AFTER THE
ACCIDENT

BOOKS BY KERRY WILKINSON

Standalone Novels

Ten Birthdays
Two Sisters
The Girl Who Came Back
Last Night
The Death and Life of Eleanor Parker
The Wife's Secret
A Face in the Crowd
Close to You

The Jessica Daniel series

The Killer Inside (also published as *Locked In*)
Vigilante
The Woman in Black
Think of the Children
Playing with Fire
The Missing Dead (also published as *Thicker than Water*)
Behind Closed Doors
Crossing the Line
Scarred for Life
For Richer, For Poorer
Nothing But Trouble
Eye for an Eye
Silent Suspect
The Unlucky Ones
A Cry in the Night

The Jessica Daniel Short Stories

January
February
March
April

Silver Blackthorn

Reckoning
Renegade
Resurgence

The Andrew Hunter series

Something Wicked
Something Hidden
Something Buried

Other

Down Among the Dead Men
No Place Like Home
Watched

KERRY WILKINSON

AFTER THE
ACCIDENT

bookouture

Published by Bookouture in 2020

An imprint of Storyfire Ltd.
Carmelite House
50 Victoria Embankment
London EC4Y 0DZ

www.bookouture.com

ISBN: 978-1-83888-516-8
eBook ISBN: 978-1-83888-515-1

AUTHOR'S NOTE

On a Friday night two years ago, British businessman Geoffrey McGinley was standing on a cliff, looking out towards the Mediterranean. He was on the island of Galanikos, a place he had visited numerous times in the past. A short while later, his unconscious body was found on the beach below.

This book attempts to unravel what happened through the eyes of the people who were there.

For reasons that will become apparent, some of the interviews for this book took place on the island close to the time of the incident. Others happened afterwards in the United Kingdom. Aside from minor edits to remove hesitations and repetitions, everything has been transcribed accurately and faithfully. Where participants opted not to give a response, this has been noted.

All names have been changed to protect those involved.

INTRODUCTION

Emma McGinley (daughter of Geoffrey McGinley): Of course I know what happened the night Dad went over the cliff.

Daniel Dorsey (business partner of Geoffrey McGinley): I'll bet Emma already told you what she thinks happened to her dad. She did, didn't she? Always full of opinions, that one. Full of herself, too. I wouldn't be so opinionated if I'd done what she'd done. She told you about that, has she? Bet she hasn't. Likes to keep it quiet. It's her mum and dad I feel sorry for. Imagine having a daughter like that and knowing what she did. I can't believe she has the brass neck to talk ill of others. I'd be keeping my head down if I were her.

Emma: He'll deny it forever – but that's just the way he is. He's never been good with telling the truth. Sometimes I wonder if he knows what truth is. It's not just that he lies, it's that he's so good at it. He convinces himself that one thing is true, even though it isn't. You read about people being able to pass lie detector tests – and I reckon he could pass one, even though we both know what he did.

Sorry, what was the question? Do I know what happened that night?

Yes. Yes I do.

CHAPTER ONE

DAY ONE

THE TRIO OF CABS

Emma: Dad was shouting into his phone. He was like the stereotypical Brit abroad. The type of guy who bellows 'English!' to some waiter, even though it's a Greek resort. I remember him talking really slowly, as if it was a child on the other end. He kept saying '*three* taxis' over and over. Then he went: 'Not *two* taxis, not *four* taxis, I ordered *three* taxis.' I was so embarrassed. We were standing on the kerb outside the airport terminal. We'd been in the country for less than an hour and I already wanted to go home.

Julius McGinley (son of Geoffrey McGinley, older brother of Emma McGinley): It was a right cock-up. The usual thing when you go abroad. Dad had ordered three taxis to pick us up at the airport and there were none there. Galanikos is an island: how much traffic can there be?

Daniel Dorsey: Total cock-up.

Emma: I'd started to walk away, then Dad shouted that the taxis would be about fifteen minutes. I think there were ten of us standing on the kerb with our cases. There was Mum, Dad, me,

Julius and the twins – that's six. Then there was Daniel and Liz, plus Victor and Claire. I still don't know why Dad invited his business partner and wife, plus their grown-up kid. I was at the point where I didn't ask too many questions.

Daniel Dorsey: Geoff said he thought of Liz and myself as family, so he asked if Liz, me, Victor and Vic's wife wanted to come along. I think it was Beth's idea. Geoff always did what Beth told him. We could hardly say no.

Emma: It was so hot. One of those days where there are no clouds in the sky and it doesn't feel like there's anywhere to hide from the sun. It had been wet in England – typical, I know – so I'd gone from that to feeling my skin tingling just from being outside. We'd been on a plane, so nobody was wearing sunscreen. I didn't want to burn.

Chloe McGinley (Aged 8. Granddaughter of Geoffrey and Bethan McGinley, daughter of Julius McGinley, niece of Emma McGinley, sister to Amy McGinley): I didn't like that Grampa was shouting. It was really hot, so I asked Dad if we could go to the shop.

Emma: There was a shop outside the terminal, selling the type of tat that you get in resorts. Julius said he wanted to get the girls out of the sun, so he took them over to the shop. I ended up following, mainly to get away from Dad.

The best thing was the air conditioning. Going inside was like being punched in the face, but in a good way – if that's a thing. A good punch in the face. That's the only reason I spent any time inside the shop because I didn't buy anything.

Right by the door, there were three spinning racks dedicated to fridge magnets, plus an entire aisle where the shelves were full of dreamcatchers. I can't believe anyone actually spends money on that stuff, but I guess they must. There were towels and plates, plus racks of booze, obviously. Chloe and Amy were dragging their dad around the shop and Julius was trying to stop them touching things on the shelves. You know what kids are like.

Chloe: I didn't touch anything!

Emma: The twins had found this necklace on a shelf close to the counter. It was made of leather twine and had these little ivory horn-shaped things stitched into it. I don't think they were *actually* made of ivory. I hope not. It was the type of thing I can imagine someone on a gap year wearing on a beach while they talk about how they've really started to get into Vonnegut.

I think it was Amy who picked it up. I'd not seen the twins in a while and, even before that, I wasn't always a hundred per cent about which was which. That sounds bad, doesn't it? Sometimes, when you look at them, it's obvious which is Amy and which is Chloe. Chloe leans forward a little more when she's speaking and Amy has this way of smiling, as if she already knows what you're about to say. I think it depends on the angle, or the light. Every now and then, I'll see them together and I can't tell who is who.

Amy McGinley (Aged 8. Granddaughter of Geoffrey and Bethan McGinley, daughter of Julius McGinley, niece of Emma McGinley, sister to Chloe McGinley): Sometimes we pretend to be each other. Even Dad gets confused sometimes.

Emma: Let's say it was Amy. She had figured out that she could blow into the horns on the necklace and it would make this whooshing sound. It's hard to describe. Julius put it on – I think as a joke – and, whenever he turned around, the necklace made the sound. Chloe and Amy thought it was hilarious.

Julius: I don't remember a necklace.

Amy: The necklace sounded like a bird whenever Dad moved about. I wonder what happened to it.

Emma: The twins were laughing, so Julius bought the necklace. It was twenty or thirty euros: a ridiculous price for what it was. I think the shop owner expected Julius to haggle – but he paid whatever the guy said. Julius has always been like that with money – make it, spend it.

Julius was putting on the necklace next to the counter but, as he was straightening, he winced, like there was a pain in his side.

Julius: Pain in my side? I don't remember anything, but it was probably just a strain, or something. I'd have got it playing five-a-side, or maybe volunteering. I'm always helping out with something.

Emma: By the time we got out of the shop, the first taxi had appeared. Dad was shouting 'three taxis' at the driver because, apparently, that makes things happen quicker. I told Mum she should get in the cab, what with her condition and everything. She said: 'Don't be so silly, I'm not dead yet.'

She was quite defiant at that point. Mum never wanted to talk about the diagnosis and basically pretended it wasn't there. She'd always been like that – putting everyone first, except herself. When we were growing up, she would always make sure that Julius and myself had eaten before she had something. I remember she once missed an Elton John concert because Dad had tickets to go to Silverstone. She loved Elton John and had always wanted to see him live – but then Dad said a mate had given him Grand Prix tickets, so they ended up going to that. She didn't even query it.

So it was no surprise that, even in the heat at the airport, she told Julius he should take the taxi to get the girls out of the sun.

I thought he'd insist that Mum should go first, but he shrugged and then got inside with the girls.

I remember looking across to Daniel and he seemed pretty annoyed by it all. He's used to getting his own way and I can't imagine him waiting for much.

Daniel: I was worried about Liz. That sun was very hot. She should have definitely been in that first cab.

Emma: Dad was marching up and down the pavement, muttering about when the next taxi would arrive. Daniel was busy doing nothing – because that's what Daniel does. I don't know what Liz and the rest were up to, but I was with Mum. It's not a busy airport, but one of those big planes took off and there was a huge roar. It was so loud, it was like you could feel it, rather than hear it. Like the whole world was quaking. I remember Mum looking up, watching the plane go overhead, and she seemed so frail and small. It was her neck where you could see it the most. There were indents and dimples, almost like she was permanently breathing in. I think that was the first time where I really, *really* understood what was going to happen to her. After you get a diagnosis like she had, it's all words at first. A doctor will say that something is going to happen, but it doesn't necessarily mean much. Then I saw her like that and it was like everything was real.

Liz Dorsey (wife of Daniel Dorsey): Beth was starting to look really thin by the time we got to Galanikos. She kept trying to say she was fine, so I didn't push her. If she wanted to talk about it, then she would.

Emma: I was trying to think of something to say – but then Mum started to talk. She goes: 'Nine years, hey? I never thought we'd be back.'

We both looked across to the terminal and the statue that sits in front. It's this giant bird-thing. A gull, maybe? When I was a girl and we used to visit, I remember that I always wanted to climb on it. It seemed so big back then, but, as I got older, I guess I realised it wasn't.

After what happened the last time we were all on Galanikos, I never thought we'd go back. I was thirty-three by the time of this holiday and so much had happened in those nine years.

It was probably the familiarity of that airport that brought it all back for Mum. We'd visited the island so many times when I was growing up – and then, after everything with Alan, we stopped.

Mum goes: 'It's nice to all be together as a family.' I suppose I'd not thought of the holiday like that until she said it. It's probably because family has never meant as much to me as it did to her.

I know that sounds bad. People will probably hate me for it – but I can't pretend to be someone I'm not. Mum loved her kids and grandkids. She enjoyed having everyone around her – but I was always happier when it was just me and her. Or, when he was in a good mood, when it was just me and Dad.

Mum once told me that she'd always wanted a huge family, five or six kids. I asked her why she'd only had two, but she never really answered. I think it was probably Dad…

Then, later, she didn't say it, but I know she'd have loved more grandkids. She adored Chloe and Amy, and she completely doted on them. She never said it out loud because that wasn't her way, but I know she'd have wanted me to try for children again. I think… um…

… Sorry, can you stop the recording? I need a minute.

Julius: Mum couldn't wait to be on holiday with the girls. She'd spent weeks telling them about the hotel, the pool and the slides. They were more excited about the all-you-can-eat buffet. Mum had told them there was unlimited ice cream and they couldn't believe it.

Emma: I didn't know how to reply to her. I don't know if she expected a response, or if she was just talking. I was thinking that I shouldn't have come, that the last thing I wanted was for everyone to be together again as a family.

I didn't tell anyone this at the time, but I deliberately chose a seat on the plane that was a few rows away from everyone else. When we all compared boarding cards, I shrugged and said it must have just worked out like that – but, really, I didn't want to be with everyone else. I couldn't stand it. I was embarrassed, if you want the truth. We used to have family get-togethers all the time – and then we didn't. It was my fault, obviously – and everyone knew it.

After all, we could hardly have had a big Sunday meal together while I was in prison.

CHAPTER TWO

THE BRAVE BOY

Emma: There was a big dinner on the first night at the hotel. It was Mum's idea, so I couldn't really say no. We were right in the middle of the restaurant, with all ten of us around this one table. I was last one down, so didn't get a choice about where to sit. The twins were at one end with Julius, while I was at the other. I had Dad on one side, Daniel on the other, and Mum opposite.

Julius: I dodged a bullet on that first night. No way was I getting stuck next to Dad and Daniel when they started knocking back the wine.

Emma: Daniel was telling this really long and *really* boring story about a skiing trip where he dislocated his shoulder. It was the type of thing you think might never end. You could circumnavigate the globe in a rubber dinghy, come back to the hotel and he'd still be banging on about it.

He was making it sound like he'd been on the beaches at Normandy, but the essence was that he'd ignored a bunch of signs, skied into a rock and fallen on his massive arse.

Daniel: Ah, the skiing trip! Did I tell you about how I dislocated my shoulder? We'd just left my villa and it was my sixth run of the day. I was on my best form until I dislocated my shoulder. Still managed to finish, mind. It was this Swiss guy's fault for not looking where he was going. I probably should've sued him, but it wasn't worth it in the end.

Emma: I asked Daniel if the doctor gave him a sticker for being a brave boy. He didn't like that.

Daniel: Emma? What would you expect from her? She always has to have the last word. I bet she didn't have such a smart mouth in prison.

Emma: I can't stand the bloke. He's one of those men that, before they've even opened their mouth, you know they're one of those 'you-can't-say-anything-nowadays'-types. The sort that goes on about winning two World Wars, even though he wasn't there for either. He'll own a massive four-wheel drive, even though he never goes anywhere near the countryside. He'll spend an hour droning on about the plague of average speed cameras on the motorway, or complaining that there's now a vegan option at his favourite pub. He'll talk about running over all cyclists, or saying how women's football shouldn't be anywhere near the TV. Not that he ever watches the lefty-liberal BBC, obviously. You think all that before he even opens his gob – then he starts talking and you realise he's everything you thought he was but much, much worse.

Sorry, where was I? Oh, yeah. Daniel Dorsey. Complete dickhead.

Julius: I knew Emma was going to blow that first night. I could see it, even from the other end of the table. She and Daniel are, um… very different people.

Emma: Daniel owns forty-nine per cent of Dad's company, so it's hard to avoid him. I try to stay away from him, but there wasn't much I could do when the only free seat was at this side. I was doing my best to ignore him, but he wouldn't shut up. I swear, that skiing story was into its second hour and he'd somehow blended it into another 'kids today' rant, which is another of his favourite moans. He was saying something about how young people always want everything on a plate, and I suppose I snapped.

Julius: Don't get Emma started about Boomers versus Millennials, or Gen X.

Emma: He kept saying how kids today aren't willing to work for anything, and how they waste all their money on phones, so I fired back at him. I said: 'Didn't you buy a bunch of council houses because the government sold them off on the cheap?' He took a breath and I think he was going to carry on as if I hadn't spoken, so I kept talking. I said: 'It's a shame young people can't do that now, isn't it? Shame that houses today are ten or twelve times' their average salary while you bought yours for eight grand.'

Julius: I don't think Emma realised that she was shouting. Everyone else had stopped and I could hear every word from the other end of the table. There was this moment of silence and then Daniel came back at her.

Emma: He said: 'That's easy to say when someone else has paid for you to be here.'

I was going to say that I only came because Mum wanted me to. He wasn't done, though. He was shouting in my face. I could see the red veins across his nose from where he's such a massive pisshead.

He goes: 'I don't think *you're* in a position to be lecturing others on morals.' Then he held up his wine glass and angled it towards me, like he's making a toast. He said something like: 'Chill out. Have a drink and enjoy yourself.'

Julius: I thought Emma was going to smack him. I looked across to this waiter who was carrying some dirty plates across towards the kitchen. He was frozen and watching, like everyone was. There was this long pause and it felt like anything could happen. Good job Mum was there.

Emma: The words were stuck, like I couldn't get out a reply. He knew exactly what he was doing when he tilted that wine glass towards me. You know that saying about 'When they go low, we go high'? Daniel is the opposite. He'll go as low as he possibly can… though not in any physical sense, of course. It's been a good two decades since he last saw his feet over that gut.

Daniel: Back in your box, little girl. Back in your box.

Emma: Dad just sat there and it was Mum who answered. She spoke really quietly – and yet it felt so powerful. Like, sometimes the quietest voice in the room is the one that talks the loudest. She goes: 'Let's not do this now.'

That put an end to it because everyone listened to her, even Daniel. Daniel gulped his wine, then turned to Julius at the other end of the table and asked something about how Julius's bank was doing. I don't remember exactly how Julius replied, but it was something like how it had been a big three months and that the only reason they'd given him the days off for the holiday was because he'd built up so much time owing.

I wish I'd listened properly now. I didn't know then that it would be important.

Julius: I don't think anyone asked about the bank.

Emma: That first dinner set the tone. It wasn't just me and Daniel, although I guess we were the loudest. Liz was moaning on about how she could only get one bar of reception on her mobile. She kept saying how it was like being in a third-world country, even though she was eating an all-inclusive buffet, while chugging down the red wine like it was water. She's the sort who'd be surprised to find out they have electricity in the north – but then she did choose to marry Daniel, so her judgement isn't the best.

Then there was Victor and Claire sitting in the middle, hardly saying anything to each other. Claire was barely eating, while Vic's plate was piled high with meat, fish, and probably a bit of everything else from the buffet.

…

I feel sorry for Vic sometimes, considering who his parents are. Then I remember that he's a forty-year-old man and that he's made his own decisions. I don't know how or why Claire married him. Julius, Vic and me are all stuck with these families – but she *chose* to marry in.

…

I suppose I'm not one to talk about making bad decisions.

Julius: Victor and Claire hated each other. No doubt about that.

Claire Dorsey (wife of Victor Dorsey): I didn't want to be at that dinner and I never should have gone on that holiday. Vic wanted a free trip and he somehow talked me into going. He said we could get our marriage back on track with a week in the sun to relax. I knew that wasn't going to happen, but I suppose I didn't see anything wrong with spending a week by the pool. More fool me, huh?

Emma: Sometimes I wonder whether everything would have been different had I been sitting next to Claire. We'd have found something to talk about and there wouldn't have been all those arguments at the very beginning.

After the row with Daniel, things calmed down for a minute or two – then Dad asked me to get him some more of the paella. I stood up to do it without thinking. Part of it was probably because I wanted to get away from Daniel – but I think there was a moment where I felt like a little girl again. When I'd been young and we'd been on the same holiday, Dad would've asked me to fill up his plate from the buffet and it felt like going back through time. Before I knew it, I was scooping rice onto a plate.

Claire: As soon as Emma headed off to the buffet, I followed. There was too much tension at that table.

Emma: Claire was standing next to me and we were making small talk about the food. Nonsense stuff, like about how the crab looked nice and all that. If someone wrote down half the stuff people make small talk about, we'd all sound completely mad.

I ended up apologising to Claire for the shouting at the table and she smiled at me, as if to say it was all right. I think I needed that.

Claire: Emma fascinated me. She seemed so nice… so normal. Perhaps the only normal one there. But then, when you know what she did, it's hard to put it all together, isn't it? I wanted to ask her about it, but I didn't know her well enough.

Emma: There were two platters of paella; one with fish and the other with pork. I got the pork one because of Dad's shellfish thing. It was an automatic thing. I barely thought about it.

Claire: I didn't know anything about Geoff being allergic to shellfish. This is the first I've heard.

Emma: It felt like Claire wanted to say something to me, but she never did. We stood there awkwardly and then we headed back to the table. Julius was still wearing that stupid necklace, and was making the twins laugh by flicking food around on a spoon. I suppose that broke the tension, even if someone was going to have to clean it up eventually.

I remember watching them and hearing the girls giggle. It was so pure – but that makes it worse sometimes.

…

I keep saying things that I know will make me sound bad.

…

I shouldn't say this, but there are times when I couldn't bear to look at the twins. I know they're my nieces, but, sometimes, being with them makes everything that happened before that feel so real. I'll be fine and then I'll hear one of them laughing and I'm back on the side of the road. It's not their fault, I know that.

Julius: Amy and Chloe only wanted to eat ice cream. I was trying to distract them.

Emma: I gave Dad his food and he said something about the hotel's paella being the best in the world. I wasn't really listening because I could still hear the twins laughing. It took me out of everything for a moment. The next thing I remember is Dad banging his ring on the side of his wine glass.

Claire: I never realised that signet ring would play such a part in my life.

Emma: It's an emerald signet ring that he always wears. Dad clinked his glass loudly enough to make everyone on the table stop talking and then he stood up. I didn't realise how much wine he'd had, but he was already slurring his words when he spoke.

He said that we were there to celebrate his and Mum's thirty-fifth wedding anniversary, plus Mum's sixtieth birthday. They both wanted everyone there and they saw Daniel and Liz as family. I suppose I wondered why Mum and Dad were paying for everything if that was the case – but it was their money and I didn't worry too much.

I can't remember what was next, but he rambled for a while and then finished by saying: 'Let's eat, drink and be merry.' He then made a *ding-ding-ding* with his ring on the glass again before he toasted the table.

Daniel: It was a good moment. Geoff always knew how to rouse the troops.

Emma: After that, Daniel pulled out a cigar and said he was off for a smoke. Dad looked to Mum, but she raised an eyebrow, which made it clear what she thought. Dad said 'maybe later' and then Daniel went off on his own.

Claire: Everything felt so much calmer after Daniel left the table.

Emma: It was only a minute or so and then Julius came across to sit in Daniel's chair. Mum said she was so happy to have the girls with us on the island. I actually felt a bit emotional hearing that. She probably thought it was the last time we'd all be together in such a place.

Julius looked towards them at the other end of the table and then said that it almost didn't happen. Simone didn't want to swap weekends with him, and the girls were due to be with her. It felt like a very deliberate thing to say, if that makes sense. Like he wasn't just talking about that week. He wanted Mum to know that Simone had always been the unreasonable one and it wasn't his fault they'd broken up.

Julius: What kind of woman would deny someone a final holiday with their grandkids? That's what Simone was like.

Extract of a letter received from Tite, Tite and Gaze Solicitors, on behalf of Simone McGinley: Allegations that my client tried to prevent her daughters from holidaying on Galanikos are a calculated, malicious and provable untruth.

Emma: That whole conversation was so weird. Julius said something about everything he did being for the girls. I can't remember the exact words, but it felt as if he'd rehearsed it. You know when somebody's heard something in a movie and they're trying to recite it back?

Perhaps it was only me who thought that? Mum took his hand across the table and thanked him for being there. It felt like a moment between them, even though I wasn't sure it was real.

Then Dad beckoned over a waiter and ordered two more bottles of wine. Start as you mean to go on, and all that.

CHAPTER THREE

THE SHOW-OFF

Emma: I'm not sure how it happened, but the men all disappeared.

Claire: I looked around the table and suddenly realised all the men had gone.

Emma: The twins were sitting next to Mum by this point and I didn't know where Julius had gone. Liz was still busy complaining about a lack of signal on her phone, while Claire was taking the chance to actually eat something after Victor had disappeared. The twins were amusing themselves, so I finally took the opportunity to ask Mum why we'd specifically returned to Galanikos.

Claire: I'd literally never heard of that island before Victor told me we were invited on a family holiday. I was really confused when I found out it wasn't *Victor*'s family holiday.

Vic said his dad's business partner used to visit Galanikos every year. There was Geoff and Bethan – plus their two grown-up kids: Julius and Emma. Julius was separated but he had twin girls. That was six of them, so that's a family, isn't it? I could just about understand Geoff and Bethan thinking of Daniel and Liz as family, given they worked together so closely. What I never really understood was why Vic and I got to go along.

Emma: Mum said we'd had loads of good times on the island before Alan died.

Claire: We were just about to take off when Vic said that someone had died on the island nine years before and that was why everyone stopped going. If we'd been getting on better, I'd have probably asked a few more questions. You talk about red flags and they're all there. I think I was seduced by the words 'free holiday' and 'all-inclusive'. It was a bit late by then anyway.

Emma: Mum said the island was her favourite place and that she might not get a chance to return. They'd given her about eighteen months to live at that point – although she never said that specifically. Perhaps it was the truth, but, even then, I thought that it was probably Dad who wanted to go back.

I remember one Christmas before I went to prison. Julius was still with Simone and I suppose everyone was happier. We'd all gone to Mum and Dad's house – and it was Dad who was talking about how great it would be to go back to Galanikos one day. I don't think Mum said anything about it.

Julius: I don't know whose idea it was to visit Galanikos specifically. It wasn't mine. Did someone say it was?

Emma: Mum has this way of shutting down when there's a subject she doesn't want to talk about. If she's into something, she'll look you in the eye and, even if she doesn't say anything, you can tell that she wants to know more. If she's said or heard enough, she'll look away and it feels like you're a naughty child being sent out of class.

When she looked away, I figured we were done. I was feeling a bit tired anyway, so said goodnight to everyone and headed into the hotel. It was probably about eight o'clock, but I don't know for sure.

I was going to flick through the TV channels and find something to send me off to sleep, but it was only when I closed the door to my room and stared at the suitcase sitting on the bed, still packed, that I realised I didn't want to be by myself.

I know there's a contradiction because I was so used to being on my own – plus I'd just walked away from a table where people would have actually talked to me. I can't really explain it. I wanted to be around people… just nobody that I actually knew.

Claire: I figured Emma had gone to bed.

Emma: I ended up going to the bar in the hotel next door. I'd ordered a Coke and was sitting by myself, watching everyone do their own thing.

I think I've always been a bit of a people-watcher. When I was at school, me and my best friend would sit high on these steps that looked out over the playground. We'd spend our whole breaks watching everyone else and talking about them. You could figure out a lot about people by keeping an eye on them when they didn't realise they were being watched… That's true in prison as well – although only if you're smart enough to not get spotted.

Paul Bosley (sound technician, Garibaldi Media): I was in the hotel bar half watching the football on TV. I can't remember which game was on, but I think it was a replay from Copa America, or something like that.

I was on my way over to the bar to get another drink when I spotted a woman sitting there. She stood out, partly because she was on her own – but also because she was so… normal. You had to be there, really. In a hotel like that, people get dressed up to go down for dinner. The women all seem to be in long dresses, with platform sandals, or heels. The guys all have dress trousers and a linen shirt. The skin tones range from light brown through to bright red. There's this unmentioned holiday etiquette in that everybody kind of looks the same.

Emma wasn't like that – although I didn't know she was called Emma then. She was wearing a baggy T-shirt with a panda on the front. It would have been normal in a café back home – but it really stood out in that bar.

Emma: I have no idea what I was wearing that night.

Paul: Emma didn't notice me at first, even though I put myself on the stool right next to her. She was busy watching everyone and I kept having to stop myself from watching her. Even *I* thought I was being creepy, but there was something hypnotic about her. She looked so out of place and yet it was also as if she belonged exactly where she was.

Emma: He kept opening his mouth as if he was going to say something and then he'd stop himself. He must have done it four or five times before I finally said: 'You can talk to me, y'know?'

Paul: If she'd not said anything, I'd probably still be giving it my best goldfish routine an hour later.

Emma: I told him my name and asked if he was on a lads' holiday. There were quite a lot of groups in that hotel, all wearing three-quarter trousers and football shirts.

Paul: I told her I was working.

Emma: I only turned to look at him properly when he told me he was working on the island. It wasn't what I expected. He said he was part of a small team that was filming a documentary. The moment he said that, the hairs went up on the back of my neck and I think I knew.

Paul: I told her there had been a death on the island nine years before, where a man had fallen off a cliff in suspicious circumstances. I remember she bit her lip for a second and then she asked what the man was called.

Emma: He told me that a businessman named Alan had gone over a cliff and that they were investigating what happened.

Paul: In retrospect, I suppose I should have realised something wasn't quite right. That's easy to say now, of course – but there was no reason for me to have suspected who she was.

Emma: I didn't tell him who I was. Not then.

Paul: Of course I fancied her. But, look, it's not like I'm one of those blokes who has the confidence to go up and talk to any girl who's by herself. I'm not someone who swipes right on everyone. I'm probably too old to be swiping in any direction.

It was one of those things. If she'd told me to get lost, or if she'd ignored me completely, then I wouldn't have said anything. She instigated the conversation. I went with it.

Emma: He was trying to show off.

Paul: I was trying to show off, if I'm honest. I thought it might impress her if I told her that I was working on a big documentary. I might have mentioned Netflix was already on board, even if they, um… well…

Emma: He said there was already a bidding war between Netflix and ITV.

Paul: I was telling her that our team looks at old mysteries, where families or friends think there might be more to an incident than was ever revealed. It was massive at the time, with *Making A Murderer*, *Serial*, *When They See Us*, that OJ thing, and all that. There was this big boom in true crime stories. I thought she'd be impressed, but she didn't seem bothered. When I later found out who she was, it seems obvious why. She had a true crime story to match any of theirs.

Emma: I let him talk. Men like to hear the sound of their own voices when they're trying to impress someone. I didn't mind.

…

Actually, that's unfair. I don't think it's just men.

Paul: I feel so stupid now. I was telling her how this businessman named Alan had slipped off a cliff and hit the rocks below. The local police called it an accident at the time, but Alan's family were never convinced – especially his son. Alan wasn't a drinker, so he wasn't drunk. He also didn't like heights, so the chances of him being on the edge of that cliff seemed slim. Alan's family had been quietly campaigning for years and arguing that the police had botched the investigation.

I was really playing it up, telling her how Alan's family was convinced it wasn't an accident and that we were there to try to uncover the truth. I kept telling her how we'd been working closely with Alan's son.

Emma: I almost said the name 'Scott' when Paul was talking about Alan's son. I guess that night would have gone differently if I'd not stopped myself.

Paul: In the end, I ran out of things to talk about. I'd been blagging it a bit anyway, probably making it sound as if I was somehow integral to this whole thing, even though I was the guy holding the boom mic. I'd probably been talking for about half an hour. I'm not usually like that, but every time I stopped, she had a question and so I was off again. My sister once told me about a series of dates she'd gone on where the blokes never stopped talking *at* her – and I suddenly realised that's exactly what I was doing.

Emma: It was my fault. I knew Paul was trying to impress me, but I never stepped in to stop him, or tell him who I was. I wanted to listen to someone else talking and he seemed happy to be there.

Paul: When I realised I'd been going on about myself almost non-stop, I asked Emma what she did. She said she worked in a shop that sold vintage clothing, which I guess explained the random T-shirt. I told her it sounded interesting and she gave me some fabulous side-eye.

Emma: I told him that I could have named any job and he'd have said he found it interesting.

Paul: That did make me laugh. She was right in that she could probably have named any career and I'd have told her it was fascinating. But it was that look that really made me feel lucky to be talking to her. A sort of half-squint with a half-smile that made it clear she wasn't for playing games. It was like she could see me… *really* see me. Does that make sense?

Emma: I didn't really want to talk about myself because there's only so long I can do that before the questions get uncomfortable. I told him I worked with my friend in a clothes shop and more or less left it at that. I didn't say that the regular hours and the routine is what saved me.

Paul: She didn't seem comfortable talking about herself and I didn't want to push. I asked if she wanted another and she said she was drinking Coke.

Emma: He gave me the look, but he didn't ask the question. I might have walked off if he had.

Paul: I didn't think it was that weird that Emma wanted a soft drink. My sister's a vegan and people are always asking her why she doesn't eat meat. It's as if *she's* the weird one for not eating things that used to be alive, even though, if you think about it, there's no reason for that to be the norm.

I figure it's quite rude to ask someone why they don't drink, why they don't eat meat, why they're not married or why they don't have kids. That sort of thing. If someone wants to tell you, they will.

Emma: He turned to me and goes: 'So what's your story? Are you single?'

Paul: She laughed, but it wasn't like she was laughing at me. It was like when you're with a mate and you take the mick out of each other.

Emma: I called him 'Mr Subtle', which he found funny. I thought about telling him I was single, or maybe even that I was married and unavailable. It was only a split second, but I decided to tell him the truth, so I said I was divorced.

Paul: I hadn't expected that. She didn't seem old enough.

Emma: He waited for a moment, probably wondering what the rest of the story was. I could've come out with something like 'We weren't compatible' and all that – but I didn't want to lie. Not then. I decided to say nothing.

Paul: She didn't want to talk about it, which was fair enough.

Emma: I liked that he didn't ask. I'd left so much unanswered, but he didn't seem bothered. So many people miss the non-verbal things. They'll either push you on things you don't want to talk about or they'll veer off and talk about something nonsensical.

Paul: I didn't know what else to talk about. I'd told her all the basics about myself and she didn't want to talk about her life. I've never been one of those people who can bring up the weather and then end up turning it into some existential conversation that will go on for hours.

Emma: I told him I should probably go – and I meant it. I stood and was genuinely ready to leave – but then I thought about inviting him to my room. It was as if the idea appeared from nowhere.

Paul: She was going to walk away and I figured I wouldn't get another chance to say something.

Emma: Before I could ask if he wanted to come back to my room, he asked if I wanted to go upstairs. I think he mentioned something about having some amazing local coffee in his room.

Paul: I'd forgotten that I mentioned coffee to her. I panicked, OK?

Emma: I thought about saying 'no', even though I almost invited him to my room. I knew he'd find out who I was eventually. I didn't want to cause trouble for him but, at the same time... it was nice to be wanted.

    …

Everyone needs that sometimes, I think. I'd not had that in a long time.

Paul: I was trying to play it cool, but I couldn't get off that stool fast enough when she said 'OK'.

Emma: I felt young in that moment. You always see yourself as an eighteen-year-old and then, suddenly, you're not any longer.

Life just disappears.

I used to go on boozy holidays with my friends when we were teenagers. We'd do shots and fishbowls – and then go back to some lad's room. There was this moment where I was able to forget about everything that had happened and could be that girl again.

Paul: I couldn't get the key card to work on my room door.

Emma: We dashed up the stairs because there was a queue for the lift. It was like being tipsy, even though I hadn't touched a drop. I think I was giggling because he couldn't get his hotel room door open.

Paul: I was inserting the card the wrong way. That's not a euphemism.

Emma: When Paul finally got the door open, I remember standing on the threshold, knowing this was my last chance to leave. A part of me wanted to – but a bigger part wanted to follow him inside.

Paul: I only realised later that everything with her dad happened while we were in my room.

Emma: I know that people said I used Paul as an alibi, but it wasn't like that. Anyone who says differently is a liar.

CHAPTER FOUR

DAY TWO

THE MAD ONE HERE

Emma: It was five or six in the morning and I was heading back into my hotel when I saw the manager coming towards me. We were in reception and he was wearing a suit, which I always thought was a harsh requirement, given the temperatures.

I didn't think anything of it until he said 'Ms McGinley'. He struggled with the pronunciation a bit, so I said to call me Emma.

He came right out with: 'It's your father' and it was like walking into a freezer. I couldn't get out a reply. He added: 'Your mother was looking for you' and then said something about the hospital.

I couldn't take it all in.

I was trying to ask questions, but he said they were waiting for me. He was pointing me towards a car that was parked outside the main doors. I don't know how long it had been waiting there, but I remember looking between the manager and the car, not knowing what to do. He said: 'Go!' and I asked if Dad was alive. He said: 'I don't know,' and then I ran to the car.

Julius: I don't think Mum had her phone, but, even if she did, there was hardly any reception at the hospital.

Emma: Someone who works at the hotel drove me to the hospital. The roads aren't very busy anyway – but they were empty at that time of the morning. I tried calling Mum but couldn't get through. Julius wasn't answering either.

It's hard to remember what I was thinking at the time – but I probably assumed he'd had a heart attack. Dad definitely drank too much and he was at that age where you start thinking about that sort of thing. The other thing was that I figured he had to be alive, else we wouldn't be going to the hospital.

It was all a bit blurry when I got there. There were loads of burnt tourists hanging around the waiting room, or people looking green or grey from too much booze. I went to the desk and asked about Dad. There was a woman who seemed like she was expecting me because she beckoned across another woman – and then I was marched through the corridors. It seemed to go on forever, one turn after another, until we eventually got to where Mum and Julius were waiting.

Julius: Emma seemed really… spaced out – plus she was wearing that same panda T-shirt from the day before. It was six or seven in the morning and she hadn't been in her room when Mum had knocked. I wondered whether she'd been drinking.

Emma: I'm not even going to dignify that with a reply. Was it Julius who said that?

Julius: The first thing she said was 'Is he alive?' Mum might have nodded, but it was me who said 'yes'. After that, Emma asked what happened. I thought it was a strange way to order things. Wouldn't you ask what had happened first if you didn't know? Dad could have been taken to hospital because he rolled out of bed – so your first question wouldn't be 'Is he alive?' Why would you assume something was that serious if you didn't know?

Emma: I don't remember what I said when I first saw Mum and Julius. I probably asked what happened. Julius then said that Dad had fallen off a cliff at the back of the hotel.

Julius: I don't think she said anything to that. She just stared.

Emma: I'd braced myself for it to be a heart attack – and then it turned out Dad had fallen off a cliff. I'd have been shocked in any case, but, because of what happened on Galanikos the last time we were there, it left me stunned. I couldn't talk.

Julius: Mum started to speak. She said that a villager had found Dad on the beach below the cliffs. The first thing Emma said was: 'Like Alan…?'

Emma: It was impossible not to think of Alan. He was Dad's original business partner until he'd fallen off a cliff nine years earlier. Then, the first time we returned to Galanikos, on night one, the same thing happened to Dad. How could anyone not be shocked by that?

Julius: It felt a bit theatrical, if I'm honest. Emma was gripping a door frame like she was trying to hold herself up. I've seen better performances on daytime soap operas.

Emma: Mum couldn't meet my eye when I mentioned Alan – but I can't have been the only one thinking how strange it was.

Julius: I was more worried about whether Dad was going to survive.

Emma: Mum said: 'You weren't in your room' – and I remember feeling like I'd been caught sneaking out of the house as a kid.

All I could manage was a simple 'No', but then she asked where I was.

Julius: I'm not sure Emma ever said where she was that night. Not at that time. I found out later.

Emma: I probably mumbled about being 'out', or something like that. It's not like I was ashamed of being with Paul, but I hardly wanted to talk about it in front of my mum or brother.

It's not as if I had a curfew. I'm a grown woman and don't have to ask for permission to go out. It was none of their business.

Julius: Emma was being evasive about where she was, but I didn't think much of it at the time. It's only later when you look back and wonder.

As for me, Chloe and Amy had been tired from the long day, the flight, and too much ice cream at dinner. I put them to bed and had fallen asleep with the TV on. It was sometime after that when Mum knocked on the door to say we had to get to the hospital. One of the deputy managers said she'd look after the girls. They were asleep anyway and I didn't want to wake them.

Emma: I'd probably only been there for a minute when the doctor came through. He said that Dad was critical but stable. He needed a machine to breathe for him and that, for now, there was little that could be done.

Julius: Critical but stable.

Emma: I have no idea what that means. If someone's critical, doesn't that indicate things are *actually* critical? I don't know how you can be stable if there's a crisis going on. If there's a burning building, you're either inside or out. There's no middle ground where it's a crisis but it's not.

Julius: Mum asked if she could see Dad and the doctor thought about it for a moment. He looked at Emma and then nodded towards Mum before saying: 'Only you.'

Emma: He said that Dad needed space and time in his condition.

Mum stood up and said she'd see us later. It was like she was asking us to leave, as if she wanted to be alone with her thoughts. I would have stayed but it didn't feel like an option. She asked me to look into flight times in case we were able to get him home, and that was it. I was only there for a few minutes. I reminded Mum that she was supposed to be resting too, but she shrugged and turned to go into the room. I think she'd forgotten that she had to look after herself.

Julius: As soon as we got into a taxi outside, Emma brought up Alan again.

Emma: We were being driven back to the hotel, but I think I was still in shock. I asked Julius why he wasn't more surprised about everything. The fact that Dad's business partner had gone off a cliff and then, nine years on, the same thing had happened to Dad. It was the whole reason we stopped visiting Galanikos and then here we were.

Julius: I didn't understand why she was so concerned about what happened nine years before, instead of worrying about how Dad was doing at that moment. We'd just been told he was critical – but she didn't want to talk about that.

Emma: Is it me? Am I the mad one here?

Julius: I stopped replying after a while and we sat in silence for the rest of the journey. Good job it wasn't a long one.

Emma: Julius paid the driver in cash when we got back to the hotel. I offered to pay, but he told me that Dad had given him some money at the airport, telling him to spend it on the girls while we were here. He said something about Dad throwing money around since Mum got her diagnosis, which I presumed was him talking about the fact that Dad had paid for Daniel, Liz, Victor and Claire to come along with us.

Julius: The manager was waiting for us when we got into reception.

Emma: I found out that the man who'd greeted me in reception was the night manager. This guy was the full manager and he knew who we both were. He asked how Dad was and, when we said he was alive, the manager put his hands together and said he'd been praying for us.

Julius: It was weird.

Emma: I thought it was really kind. He said we were now his honoured guests and that there was a pair of cottages at the back of the property we could have. There would be a lot more privacy and shade back there, so he'd already arranged to have Mum and Dad's things moved to one of the cottages. He was asking what we wanted to do with the other.

Julius: I knew Emma wanted that second cottage. Not only that, she'd sulk if she didn't get it. She was always like that as a kid. I once got this big Lego set for Christmas, where you could build a car. Emma started crying because she decided that's what she wanted. She'd already had loads of presents, but Mum ended up buying her the same set as mine as soon as the shops opened again.

When the manager mentioned two cottages, I didn't think it was worth arguing.

Emma: I don't know why Julius turned down that cottage. I told him that the girls would love it, but he insisted he wanted to stay in the main hotel. There was something about the girls liking the view of the pool, but I thought it was probably more about him than them. He said that Mum was going to need someone nearby and that it might as well be me. That was probably closer to the truth: he didn't want to deal with any potential hassle from Mum.

I certainly wasn't going to let Daniel and Liz take it, so I said I'd move my things down. The manager started waving his hands, saying there were bellboys who would help, but I told him I only had one bag that I hadn't unpacked.

Julius: Emma got her way. There's a surprise.

Emma: When I got back downstairs with my bag, the manager took me out to the back of the hotel. I couldn't believe it at first. I'd pictured some sort of run-down staff quarters – but the cottages were beautiful. There was a perfect green lawn at the front, with neat flower beds on both sides. The two buildings were symmetrical, with a red door in the centre of each and a window on the side. They were hidden away behind a hedge and I assumed that was where the property line sat. They were so shiny that it was almost as if they'd been painted the day before.

The manager showed me to the door of the one he said was mine and it was so lovely that I felt embarrassed to be walking in there when it was just me and my bag. Everything was sparkling, like a whole team had gone in and scrubbed everything until it was impossible to be any cleaner. There were thick marble counters and big sliding doors at the back. It's definitely the nicest place I've ever slept.

Julius: Did she tell you about the marble counters? She told everyone else.

Emma: I felt so overwhelmed by it all. It didn't feel right that Dad had almost died and I was benefitting because of it. Then I had to gulp away tears because the walls of my cell suddenly felt so close. Anyone who's been in prison will tell you that it never really goes away. It might be a clang that reminds you of the doors closing, or a squeak that makes you think of someone moving in the bunk above or below. The screech of cutlery is the worst for me. If I ever hear a knife scrape on a plate, I'm back at mealtimes.

As I was looking around this lovely space, all I could think about was how different it was to the place where I'd been not that long before.

Julius: I probably should have taken the cottage.

Emma: I was still in the same clothes from the day before, so, after the manager left, I locked everything up, put down the blinds and then went and had a shower.

I remember standing under the water, thinking it was the best shower I'd ever had. I know that's strange, but I think it was the water pressure. I was standing there, letting the water thump into me, and I felt so… clean. I couldn't tell you how long I was in there. I honestly think I could have fallen asleep in there.

Julius: I almost went back to reception to have the manager open the cottage door and check on Emma. She wasn't answering the door and I still couldn't be sure about whether she had been drinking the night before.

Emma: I didn't hear Julius knocking on the cottage door. The shower is at the back and I had everything closed in between. The water would have been loud – and then I had to get dressed. I was surprised when he said he was on the brink of going to get the manager to check on me.

Julius: I was worried about her. That's the thing with Emma. You try to do something for her and, instead of acknowledging the gesture, she tries to second-guess everything and wonders if you have an ulterior motive.

Despite everything she did, and despite what happened on the island, I'm still her older brother.

Emma: When we'd established that I'd simply been in the shower, Julius asked if I'd like to babysit the girls that night. When we were on the way back from the hospital, we'd sort of been arguing without actually arguing, so I wondered if there was something behind it all.

Julius: Told you: always trying to second-guess everything.

Emma: He said the twins had missed seeing me and that he wanted me to be a part of their lives. I didn't know what to say at first because I hadn't been alone with a child since I got out of prison.

…

It wasn't a part of my release conditions, or anything like that. It's not like I'm a danger to kids – but people look at you differently when you've done what I did. I understand it and I don't blame anyone but myself.

What Julius said did make me feel a bit teary, if I'm honest. I think I embarrassed both of us because Julius started speaking really quickly, saying that I'd be doing him a favour because he could get out of the hotel for a bit.

I told him I'd definitely look after the girls. I was looking forward to it – and, just for a moment, it felt like that island was the best place for me. I suppose I momentarily forgot about what had gone on with Dad.

Then he said that someone had to go and update Daniel and Liz about what had happened – and I realised he meant me.

Julius: I know Emma doesn't like Daniel, but it's not as if I'm his biggest fan, either.

Emma: Julius and I found Daniel and Liz by the pool. They had their towels spread across about six beds and Liz was sipping away on a cocktail, even though it was breakfast time. Chloe and Amy were on the edge of the pool, but it didn't look as if anyone was paying them much attention.

Julius told them to go and play on the slides for a bit, but they didn't want to. I'd have been the same if I knew something bad had happened and nobody was telling me. Sometimes I think it's better to treat children with maturity, rather than trying to tiptoe around them. Kids can be so resilient and if you try to hide things from them, it breeds mistrust and perhaps even a fear of the unknown.

…But then I guess I'm not the person to be giving parenting advice.

Julius: Emma did the talking.

Emma: I told them that Dad had fallen off the clifftops behind the hotel and that he was unconscious in hospital. I used that 'critical but stable' line, which they nodded along to. I don't think they understood it any more than I did.

I thought they'd ask a bunch of questions. It's not as if I had many answers but, when it came to it, they hardly said anything.

Julius: I think Daniel said something like 'That's terrible' – and then Liz parroted him.

Emma: Daniel asked how long he was likely to be in hospital and I said that I didn't know. He was still unconscious at the moment.

Julius: They both seemed really distant about everything, as if Emma had told them that Dad had a cough and was going to be late down.

Emma: Apart from sitting up a bit, I don't think either of them moved. Liz even gulped down another mouthful of her cocktail.

Julius: I was definitely expecting more of a reaction.

Daniel: To be honest, it was the way she said it. She mumbles a lot. I thought she meant Geoff had been on the cliff and twisted his ankle, something like that. I didn't think she was talking about an actual fall *from the top*. I was shocked when I found out later on. Liz will back me up on this.

Liz: Did you already ask Dan that question? I agree with whatever he told you.

Emma: It was almost as if they hadn't heard me. Then Daniel looked sideways to Liz and pushed himself up so that he was sitting properly. He said he was sorry for the argument we had the night before and that he hadn't meant anything he said.

Daniel: That girl should have been the one apologising, but I wanted to be the bigger man. I didn't want her bringing me down to her level and spoiling Liz's holiday.

Emma: It was obvious he didn't mean a word of it. He didn't take off his sunglasses and I doubted he could even remember what he'd said to me the night before, let alone when he'd toasted me with that glass. I remember his exact words at the end. He coughed and then said: 'When I said "Have a drink", I didn't mean…' before he tailed off.

He never finished the sentence, so I did it for him. I told him: 'I know exactly what you meant.'

He lifted his sunglasses and looked at me properly and there was this sort of surprise there. It's obvious that we don't like each other, but I really think he believed this non-apology would do the trick. That you can say and do whatever you like and then wave it away afterwards. He was shocked that I wasn't accepting it.

Julius: It's not like Emma and I are best mates – but even I know that wasn't an apology.

Daniel: I had nothing to say sorry for. I only did it for Liz. I'm still waiting for *my* apology. Look at what I've done with my life and what she's done with hers and tell me who you believe.

Emma: I didn't want to be there any longer and knew we'd end up having another argument if I didn't leave. I noticed that Claire and Victor were set up on the other side of the pool, so I left Julius with the girls and went around to them.

Daniel: She stomped off. Don't know what her problem was.

Emma: Claire and Victor were on sunbeds right next to each other – but they were angling in opposite directions. They were like two pieces from different puzzles.

I told them what happened to Dad the night before and got more of a normal reaction from them. Claire said something like 'Oh my goodness', while Vic said that Dad was a chuffing good bloke and a right, jeffing inspiration to him.

Claire: I had to tell Vic to mind his language because there were kids right in front of us. He was always oblivious to things like that.

Emma: Claire immediately asked if there was anything she could do. I told her she could probably talk to Julius because he might need a bit of help with the girls if we all had to visit the hospital. She said that wouldn't be a problem.

I kind of wished Vic wasn't there because I think Claire and I might have had a proper conversation. From the meal the night before, I'd seen that she was a lot freer without him. Whenever they were together, it was like she was guarding herself. I thought about sitting down by her anyway – but I suppose if I'd done that, I wouldn't have noticed what happened next.

Daniel: The pool thing? Are you joking?

Emma: I was on my way back to the cottage, but I had to pass Daniel and Liz on the way. Julius had disappeared by this point. There was this guy walking around the pool wearing a suit – and it was obvious he wasn't a tourist. He said something about a 'best deal' and then passed me a card, like people sometimes do when you're outside a supermarket, or wherever. It's usually a coupon, or some sort of advert. This was for a car rental place a few streets away from the hotel. I was probably going to bin it – but I didn't want to do it in front of him, so I ended up thanking him and holding onto it.

I didn't know his name at the time, although I learned later it was Barak. He carried on for a few steps and then stopped in front of Daniel. He held his hands wide and goes: 'Good to see you again, Mr Dorsey.'

Daniel: It was all a misunderstanding. That's what happens when people can't speak proper English.

Emma: Barak's English was really good, but he definitely had an accent. That didn't stop me hearing what he said.

Daniel isn't one of those men who can hide his feelings. If he's angry, his chest starts heaving and his face goes red. That's exactly what happened when he looked back to Barak and replied: 'I think you're mistaken. We've never met. I've never been to this island.' It was all through gritted teeth.

Daniel: I'd never met that man before in my life and I'd certainly never visited Galanikos before that trip.

Emma: Barak looked so confused, as if he was a puppy whose owner had left him outside a shop. This mix of hurt and bemusement.

Daniel snatched away a card and then Barak moved onto the other side of the pool. I watched him as he went and he kept looking back towards Daniel, wondering what had just happened.

Daniel: That girl's deluded if she told you that.

Emma: I was wondering what had just happened – then Daniel leapt up and pulled a cigar from his back pocket. He didn't say anything, just marched away towards the smoking area.

Liz: It was all a big misunderstanding. I think I'd know if my husband had gone on holiday.

Emma: Misunderstanding, my arse.

CHAPTER FIVE

THE SINGLE TRAFFIC CONE

Emma: I went back to my cottage after the incident with Daniel at the pool. Mum had asked me to look at flights off the island, but there didn't seem much point, considering Dad was still unconscious.

I didn't want to spend time around the pool because it seemed like Daniel and Liz were camped there for the day, plus I wasn't in the mood. I decided to go for a walk instead.

We'd visited the resort enough times when I was younger, so I had a good idea of where everything was. I also wanted to see how things had changed in the nine years since we'd last been.

Since we'd landed, it had been one thing after another and I thought it might help clear my head.

Julius: I don't know what happened to Emma later that morning.

Emma: I remember the first ever holiday I went on. I was about five and it was in a caravan at the seaside. Dad drove and Julius and I were in the back of the car. Julius would have been about ten or eleven and couldn't sit still. We were giving it the full 'Are we there yet?' treatment and we'd play I-Spy or these made-up games about spotting number plates, or certain colours of car. It felt like the journey went on for most of the day, but it was probably a couple of hours at most.

I don't remember much more about the holiday other than that everything felt really cramped in the caravan. We'd all be climbing over one another whenever we had to move around.

When I got back to school, people asked about where I'd been on holiday. I told them about the caravan and everyone laughed.

…

Maybe not everyone, but that's how it felt. These girls would be talking about how they'd been to France, or Italy. Someone had been to Switzerland and I didn't even know where that was at the time. It sounded like a made-up country.

I suddenly realised that we were poor. Before that, I obviously knew that some kids had things that I didn't – but I don't think I ever understood that the big divider was poor kids versus rich kids.

It feels like something so distant now. Sometimes I wonder if they are false memories – but I know they're not. That was my life at the beginning.

It must have only been a year on from that when everything changed. I'd not done anything, but I was suddenly one of the rich kids. It was all because of Dad. I didn't understand what he'd done for a while, other than that it was something to do with buying houses.

Then we came to Galanikos for the first time.

The hotel was the first major building in the resort and we were one of the first visitors. The iron curtain had come down and flights were starting to get cheaper. The other rich kids at school were still talking about France or Italy – but now I had something on them. I had this exotic place, far away from anything any of us could imagine.

It felt like this island was *my* island.

Mum and Dad came here every summer and so did I for a long time. I missed a few trips when I was in my late-teens and went away with my friends instead – but I was here for most of them.

… That all stopped nine years ago, when Alan went off that cliff. He and Dad were in business from back when they started putting their money together to buy run-down houses. Maybe twenty years? Something like that.

There was a big fall-out after that last trip and I never thought I'd see this place again.

I didn't think I wanted to be on the island again – but then I walked out of the hotel on that morning after Dad had fell – and I was that little girl again.

Galanikos was suddenly this place of wonder once more.

I thought about going down to the village itself but wanted to save it as a treat. Instead, I walked around the side of the hotel out towards the cliffs. There's an amazing view where you can stand near the edge and stare out across the ocean. There's nothing in the way: no trees, no rocks, no other islands. It's like the view goes on forever, with the blue of the ocean driving deep towards the horizon and then disappearing into the sky.

The sun rises on that side and, if you get up early enough, you can watch the night turning purple, orange and red before it fades to blue.

…

I say: 'If you get up early enough' – but the only times I've seen that is when I stayed up through the night. I was younger then…

Julius: I've watched the sun rise on that cliff – I think most tourists have. If not there, then you can see the sun set from the beach on the other side. It's one of the top-ten things they list in the guidebook for people to experience. But once you've seen one sunrise, you've seen them all.

Emma: When I saw what was on the clifftop that morning, I almost laughed. There was a single traffic cone sitting close to the edge. That was how they'd marked the place where Dad had fallen. I thought about all the people who complain about health and safety culture in the UK – and what they'd make of it. Would even the solo cone be too much for them?

There was a man standing close to that cone with his back to me. I could see the smoke from his cigarette drifting away and assumed it was someone from the hotel who had snuck out for a smoke. It was only when I got across to the cliff edge that I realised I knew him.

I honestly think he was wearing the same black trousers from nine years before. They were the sort you'd wear to an office – but way too baggy on him. He had on this plain white shirt but had sweated through the sides and it was all so familiar. The same man wearing the same clothes – but nine years apart.

Jin turned to me, looked me up and down, and then spun back to the ocean. 'Ms McGinley,' he said. 'Fancy seeing you here.'

I think he was trying to make a joke, but it didn't feel like that.

'Jin' (Galanikos head of police): I didn't think they would ever be back. Would you, after what happened the last time?

Emma: I never knew whether 'Jin' was his first name, last name, or a nickname. It was pronounced like the drink and that's what he told everyone to call him. He was the head of police when Alan had fallen and it looked like he was still doing the job.

We were standing side by side and I followed his stare along the coast towards the cliff from where Alan fell. It's a little further away from the hotel, where there's a path that winds down to the beach below. Alan landed on rocks, while Dad had apparently been found on the sand.

Neither of us said anything for a while, but it did feel as if there was a connection. Like we were in the same place and thinking the same thing.

Then he said it.

Jin: 'Here we go again.'

Emma: It was flippant but not mean. I knew where he was coming from.

After Alan fell, Jin got a lot of abuse for apparently 'botching' the investigation. I imagine that all took a long time to die down. He might have thought his career was over. Then we come back after all this time and, yeah… Here we go again.

Jin: I told her what time her dad had been found – and asked where she was for the hours before that.

Emma: I said I was in a bar. He wanted to know if I was with anyone, so I said 'yes', without giving a name. He didn't push for more and didn't write anything down. It wasn't a serious inquisition.

Jin: I can't talk about who was a suspect and who wasn't.

Emma: I asked why there was no fence.

Jin: It's never the locals who fall.

Emma: I didn't like it when he said that. It was dismissive, as if the tourists who come to the island don't mean anything. That they're the only ones stupid enough to fall.

Jin: Who would pay for this fence? Do you know how long it would have to be? If you don't want the danger, don't go near the edge. Everyone who lives here manages to figure that out.

Emma: He'd annoyed me, which is why I told him that he'd have to do some work to find a real suspect this time. I knew what I was saying. I wanted a reaction, but he continued staring out over the ocean.

Jin: She knows nothing.

Emma: When Alan fell, the only named suspect was Dad. That wasn't based on anything particular, simply that there was a small discrepancy about times – and that Jin didn't want to do his job. There was no evidence, which is why no charges were ever laid.

It had made the news back home and, because Dad had been named, the rumours took a long time to go away. It's no wonder people say the investigation was botched. It ended up concluding that Alan had simply fallen – but, by then, there was already talk about business feuds and the like.

Jin: Your system is not our system. People said we had a small mentality, that your way is better, but there was no problem with my investigation. No problem at all.

Emma: As soon as Jin finished that one cigarette, he moved onto the next. I said I thought Dad must have been pushed. It was mainly because I couldn't see a way Dad would have fallen, not after what happened with Alan. Why would he be right on the edge? Nothing made sense.

Jin: I told her: 'Maybe he jumped?'

Emma: There was no reason for Dad to do that. He was happy, not suicidal. It was offensive that Jin even said it. He then added: 'Funny you seem to know what I think'.

I didn't know what to say about that. It felt like a challenge: a way of telling me to stay out of his way. I was ready to go, but then he called me back.

Jin: I said I'd seen Lander that morning – because I had.

Emma: I know what he was trying to do when he said that. He wanted to show that he still held something over me, even though he didn't.

I'd not heard Lander's name in a long while and I waited for a moment, wondering if he had something else to say. Jin gave me a card and told me to call if I thought of anything. He said he hoped Dad recovered – and I walked away.

Jin: That was the first time anyone mentioned a push. It was her, on that cliff, the morning after.

CHAPTER SIX

THE SMELL OF HOPE OR SEWERS

Emma: I walked down the path, away from the edge and that stupid cone. I thought about heading back into the hotel, but it was late in the morning and the scent of the village was in the air. It's always the smells that get me.

Not long after I'd been released, I'd gone into a mall where the cleaners were busy working. They were using this detergent that must have been the same one from prison. I was frozen in front of the door, unable to shift until someone asked if I could move. I bet I could smell that again in thirty years and it would still send me right back in time.

That's what it was like when I was outside the hotel. I was helpless to do anything other than follow my nose down the slope towards the centre of the village. It was déjà vu the entire way, remembering how I used to feel making this journey. I was a young woman then, a girl even, and I had my whole life ahead of me. This time, it felt like so much of my life was behind me. I'd wasted those best years and, if anything, gone backwards.

Julius: Emma always had a thing about the village below the hotel. I didn't see it myself. The hotel was about as luxurious as you're going to get on an island like that, so why waste your time in a dump?

Emma: Things must have changed over time, but, as I got to the edge of the market, it all seemed the same as I remembered. There were the stalls selling counterfeit football shirts, bags and branded tops. The rug stall was still on the corner, with a huge, faded carpet rolled up against a telegraph pole. I swear it was like that the last time I'd seen it.

I suppose the sights are much like any market – but it's the smell that sets it apart. It's hard to describe because you have to experience it. It starts at some time after eleven, when the locals are cooking lunch, hoping to entice the tourists. There are these huge vats of rice, vegetables and spices, which blends with fresh fish being grilled on outdoor barbecues. Because the village sits down a path below the hotel, it all whips together on the breeze and drifts its way up.

It's just…

…

It's the smell of hope and being young. Summer and sun. There's nothing like it.

Julius: I don't think I've ever noticed a smell. Sometimes the sewers run over. Is that what you're talking about?

Emma: I ended up sitting at a table outside a café. There was shade and a gentle breeze. All I wanted to do was watch and listen. To absorb everything. I had a lump in my throat and cried a little bit to myself.

I'd usually have found a place to be alone and hide everything – but I didn't want to move in case the feeling went away. It was the village that caused that. It was that smell.

I could tell you I was upset about Dad, but it wouldn't be true… not completely. It was those feelings of the life I'd lost.

At the sentencing, my solicitor talked about 'genuine remorse' and it always stuck with me. He said: 'She has genuine remorse for what happened' and it felt like one of those things a lawyer would say. I bet everyone has 'genuine remorse' because it makes their sentences shorter. Except, I was actually broken by it.

Properly broken.

I could barely dress myself, or get out of bed. I wasn't eating. I had to be reminded to drink. People would whisper about me and wonder if I was planning to kill myself.

And, as I sat outside that café, all I could think about was how younger me had walked through this village, had drunk the tea and eaten the fish. How she'd never have been able to guess the person I'd become.

So, yeah, I cried for myself.

Julius: I don't think I visited the village once on that trip. Why would I?

Emma: We went to the island so often that it would have been impossible not to pick up a little of the local dialect. I'm not saying I'm bilingual, but I do know the odd word and sentence, plus I can generally get the gist of what someone means.

I was sitting at that table and there were these two men standing near the café door talking to each other. I heard the word 'beach' and 'fall', plus what I thought was the word 'British'. I turned around and asked the man who was talking if he was the person who'd found Dad on the beach.

He only knew a few words of English, but we managed to figure it out through a mixture of the two languages.

I told him I was staying at the hotel and that my dad had fallen the night before. He came across and held my hand. He knew the word for 'sorry' and kept saying it, before the café owner had to help us piece together the next bit.

He was saying a word that sounded like 'smock'. I'm probably pronouncing it wrong. The owner was saying 'fall', 'fall' – and I didn't get it. I felt like such an idiot because what he was trying to say was that the man hadn't just found my dad on the beach, he'd seen him fall.

Julius: Sometimes Emma hears what she wants to hear.

Emma: The man said he was walking on the beach and heard a noise from up on the cliffs. It was dark by then, so he didn't realise what was happening. He saw a shadow and thought it might have been a tree branch falling. It was only when he got closer that he realised it was a person… that it was Dad.

He said he'd already talked to Jin about it that morning because he was sure the noise he'd heard from the cliff wasn't just a voice. He said it was *voices…*

CHAPTER SEVEN

THE STUPID SENSE OF ENVY

Emma: I can't remember how I felt when I was walking up the hill from the village. I've been on that beach and, when it's quiet, it's almost as if it absorbs all the noises from around and above. You can hear boats from the other side of the island, or chatter drifting from the village. Perhaps he had heard voices from above – but that wasn't proof Dad was with someone.

It also wasn't proof that he was alone.

Claire: It was sometime on the morning after Geoff fell that I went for a walk on my own. I didn't know the layout of the island but ended up on the beach underneath the cliff. I was following one of the paths at the side of the hotel, wondering where it went. I'd not necessarily planned to be there.

The main thing I remember is how noisy it was down there. It was this little cove that seemed like it was sheltered by the cliff. You'd think it would be this peaceful postcard, but, instead, it was like all the sounds from the island converged there. There were birds chirping and car engines rumbling. There was nobody anywhere near me, but it felt like I was in a crowd. Then, as immediately as it began, the wind dropped and there was silence. It was the creepiest thing I've ever known.

Emma: To get to the cottage, I had to walk around the pool. I wasn't paying much attention to anything and certainly didn't want to accidentally catch Daniel's eye. I was almost past the area where they stack sun loungers when I realised Mum was sitting on the edge of a bed next to Daniel and Liz, close to the water.

Liz: Beth got back from the hospital and not one of her kids were there for her. Good job she had us.

Emma: I went across and asked how she was. She looked so tired. I know that shouldn't have been a surprise because she'd spent the night at the hospital – but it was deeper than that. I think you can tell the difference when you see people. Someone might look like they need a good night's sleep, but, other times, it's like their eyes haven't closed in days. Their whole face hangs and there's a small delay when they try to talk, as if you're in different time zones.

When I asked Mum how she was, it took a second for her to blink her way up to me and open her mouth. She said she was 'all right', but only in the way people do when they don't know what else to say. I think it's a British thing, almost like our national catchphrase. Someone could have been hit by lightning and crawled their way across a county to the nearest hospital and then, when a doctor asks how they are, they'd say 'all right'. It's what people do. It's what I said when Mum visited me in prison for the first time.

I asked about Dad and she said he was breathing for himself now and making progress, even though he was still unconscious. I think she'd forgotten that she asked me to look for flights because she never mentioned it.

Liz: Beth just wanted a rest. She'd been up all night, the poor thing. Instead of leaving her be, Emma kept on at her, asking how she was, how Geoff was, all that. I wanted to tell her to go away, but it wasn't my place.

Emma: Mum said she was going back to the hospital later in the afternoon and asked if I wanted to go with her. I told her that of course I would.

Liz: It was obvious to anyone watching that Emma didn't want to go. Beth put her on the spot, where she couldn't say no.

Emma: I asked Mum what she thought of the cottage – but she didn't know anything about it. I had to tell her that the manager had moved all her things to a private cottage, instead of the main hotel. Nobody had told her and, when she got back from the hospital, she'd gone straight to the pool.

I ended up walking with her around the back of the pool out towards the cottages. That's when I noticed the flowers.

Julius: I only saw it later. The staff had put together this display of flowers next to the door of Mum's cottage. Fair play to them.

Emma: Someone had put in a lot of effort. They'd woven the flowers into a heart shape and then rested it up against the wall. Mum burst into tears the moment she saw it. She kept saying how kind it all was, but I was more worried about her physically. I was having to hold her up because she was so frail. I ended up guiding her over to the door and then I let her in with the key that the manager had left me.

It was a lot cooler inside because of the air con, but Mum was like a ghost. She was drifting aimlessly around the room while constantly catching herself on the corners of things. She barely seemed to notice and I did wonder if she'd taken something. I didn't want to ask.

She said she wanted to take a shower, so I left her doing that while I waited in the bedroom area. There was a king-size bed and I remember thinking that Mum was going to find it very empty when it came to sleeping. She was having a hard enough time of it as it was – and that was before what happened to Dad.

…

I realise I contributed to everything that went wrong.

Julius: After Emma got her sentence, she wasn't around to see how Mum took it. I would sometimes take the girls round to their house and Mum would still be in bed, even though it was the afternoon. Other times, she'd be on a cleaning spree and would be doing something like scrubbing the floor of a cupboard. I never knew which version of her would be home when I visited.

I know Emma will say she had it tough inside… but it was hardly a party outside.

Emma: When Mum came out of the shower, she said she wanted to sleep but made me promise to wake her at four o'clock, so that she could go back to the hospital. I told her I would, then she slipped a tablet and got herself under the covers. I didn't even ask what she'd taken.

Julius: Mum took a lot of pills during the time Emma was inside. She tried to hide them at first, but it became too obvious. I would have asked what they were – but it wouldn't have made any difference. I think we've always been a family of people who do what they want – and only answer questions if we need to.

Emma: I don't know what I did for the next few hours. I might have slept myself… but that doesn't sound like me. Perhaps I went for another walk? I doubt I went to the pool. Do you really need to know?

Julius: I don't think I saw Emma between the time we got back from the hospital and later that night. It's only now, looking back, when I wonder where she was, or – perhaps more importantly – who she was with.

Emma: When I woke Mum, she was looking a little better – but not much. There were still rings around her eyes and that hollowed sense that she carried. We ended up getting another taxi to the hospital and then the receptionist there waved us through. They knew who she was by then and I think word had gone around the island about what had happened.

Mum knew where she was going and led the way through the corridors without anyone stopping us. It would have probably felt odd, except that it all happened so fast that I didn't have time to think it over. Before I knew it, we were in front of a door and a nurse was waiting for us. She said that Dad was doing as well as could be expected – and a few other things that I don't really remember.

After that, she showed us inside. Dad had a private room to himself. It was quite a big space, all white, with a bed right in the middle. He was lying on his back in the bed, with the sheets tucked underneath his chin. Mum went closer to the bed, but I watched as he breathed in and out. It was so… *peaceful*.

I remember this stupid sense of envy; that I'd love to be able to sleep like that. I knew it wasn't *real* sleep, that he was in a coma, but my mind was all over the place.

Mum was sitting at his side and she'd taken his arm out from under the covers. She was talking to him, saying she was there and that she loved him. She was holding his hand, squeezing his fingers and I felt so out of place. I shouldn't have been there. I had no idea what I could say to him, whether he was awake or not.

Yes, he's my dad, but I broke a part of him when I broke a part of me. How do you take that back?

I felt out of the moment, distant and detached, almost out of my body.

It's funny how things like that happen. How you can sit and stare at a problem that never goes anywhere and then, the moment you step away, the answer slips into your mind.

I think that's probably why I saw what wasn't there, instead of what was.

Dad's ring was missing.

CHAPTER EIGHT

THE WRONG THING TO SAY

Emma: Mum stared at Dad's hand and then looked back up to me. She goes: 'He never takes it off,' which I already knew. That emerald signet ring was almost the thing for which Dad was best known. If he had to knock on someone's front door, he'd do it with that ring instead of his knuckles. He sometimes used it to flick the cap off bottles. It was like he'd made it a part of himself.

He had definitely been wearing it the night before because he'd dinged his glass and made that speech.

Mum checked his other hand and then spoke to a couple of people at the hospital to see if Dad had been brought in alongside any other possessions. They said he hadn't.

I know he'd fallen, but it seems unlikely gravity would be enough to remove a ring from someone's fingers, which left us both thinking he might have been robbed. That made a lot more sense than him simply falling.

I still had Jin's card on me, so tried calling the number he'd given. I wanted to tell him about Dad's missing ring – but there was no answer. I probably tried three or four times, before leaving a message to ask if we could speak.

Jin: I had things to do. There was another big thing happening at that time.

Emma: I left Mum alone with Dad for a bit – but visiting hours were almost over, so it wasn't long before we got a taxi back to the hotel. Dinner had started, but Mum had asked if everyone could wait for us, because she wanted another group meal.

Julius: The girls were hungry and trying to make them wait for Mum to get back from the hospital wasn't going down well. It's partly my own fault for letting them have so much ice cream on the first night.

Emma: Dinner on night two was a lot quieter than night one. Not a surprise after what happened to Dad.

Julius: It helped that Daniel and Emma were at opposite ends of the table.

Emma: Everything was quiet and pleasant. Liz asked something about the possibility of visiting Dad in hospital, but Mum said there were limited slots, so they might as well continue to enjoy the holiday. If it had been anyone except Mum saying it, I would've thought it was a little dig about them spending all day at the pool. I don't think she meant it like that, though.

Liz: Daniel was really worried about Geoff – we both were. We'd have done anything to help.

Emma: Things were winding down when Daniel got up to leave. He held a cigar up in the air as if that explained everything. It was one of those giant Bratwurst-like things, the sort of expensive one you only ever see fat, rich men puffing away. They act like massive dicks, so they might as well practise sucking on one, I guess.

He disappeared out of the restaurant and I didn't think much of it. That's when Mum told me I should eat more.

Julius: I heard that. Definitely the wrong thing to say.

Emma: I ignored her at first, pretending I hadn't heard – then she spoke louder. She said: 'You got so thin when you went away. You can eat anything you want here.'

Julius: Mum would never say Emma had been to prison. She'd always talk around it, saying she'd 'gone away', or 'had things to do'. That was probably the weirdest. Simone and I were trying to be honest with the girls, but then Mum would say Emma had 'things to do' and it would confuse them even more.

Emma: I had a bit of rice on my plate, perhaps some fish. I wasn't hungry but also didn't want to argue for a second night in a row, especially in the circumstances. I said I'd had a large lunch, which was a lie, though Mum didn't know that. There was an irony in that I had been telling her to look after herself, but there she was saying the same to me.

Julius: The girls were excited because Auntie Emma was going to look after them that night. After Simone and I split, I always tried to create events for them to look forward to. When it was my weekend with them, I'd let them know in advance where we were going so they'd want to see me. That holiday was all about setting little goals. They could swim in the morning, go to the beach in the afternoon, or have ice cream in the evening. That sort of thing.

I'd not told them properly about what happened with Dad, only that he'd had a fall and was poorly in hospital. They didn't know about the coma, or how serious it was. I wanted to keep their minds off it, so that whole day was about the build-up to their evening with Emma.

Emma: The girls were getting more and more excited as we had dinner. One of them would say: 'Are you going to let us stay up until nine?' If I said I would, the other would ask if it could be nine-thirty. It probably didn't help that Julius let them go back for a third bowl of ice cream each.

Julius: When they were two or three, Emma bought the twins a squeaky hippo each for their birthday. Those hippos were so loud, you could hear them through walls. You could hear them in the garden when they were inside a locked house. Emma might have forgotten, but I hadn't. If the girls wanted three bowls of ice cream, then three bowls it was.

Emma: As everyone was finishing, Julius went to take the girls upstairs into the hotel. I told him I'd be up in about twenty minutes but that I had to grab a few things from the cottage first. Really, I wanted to wash my face and have a little rest.

Mum said she hadn't finished eating, so I left her at the table with Liz, and then headed past the pool towards the cottages.

Liz: Left her Mum all alone. Tells you something, doesn't it?

Emma: I had let myself into the cottage and was on my way into the bathroom when I heard footsteps from the back…

…

Actually, the more I think about it, the more I don't think it *was* footsteps. There was grass at the back and I don't think I'd have heard someone walking unless they were being really loud. I heard *something*, though – which is why I let myself out the sliding door at the back. That's when I saw Daniel peeping into Mum's cottage.

CHAPTER NINE

TINA

Daniel: That's slander. Or libel. Or both.

Emma: Daniel was peering through the window at the back, but I wonder now if the sound I heard was him trying the door.

Daniel: Absolutely, one hundred per cent, not true.

Emma: When he saw me, it was like he was a kid caught in the fridge after midnight. He held up his cigar, which he hadn't lit, and said he was looking for somewhere to smoke. It might have been more believable if the hotel's only smoking area wasn't in the opposite direction. He knew that because he'd gone there the night before.

Daniel: I asked one of the little server fellows where I could smoke – and that's where he pointed me. If you want to take it up with anyone, take it up with him.

Emma: I told him the smoking area was in the same place it had been the night before. The same place he'd gone that morning. He stared back at me for a second and I know he was trying to think of a better explanation for why he'd been snooping. In the end, he disappeared off towards the place he should have been.

Daniel: You should be asking her about why she was staying in that cottage in the first place. Her dad had an accident and, somehow, she benefitted from it. There's a whole lot of questions I'd have for her, if it was me.

Emma: I watched him go and followed him around the front. He kept turning and looking at me and it definitely felt good to have him on the run.

Daniel: There's something wrong with that girl.

Emma: I waited until Daniel had gone and then went back into the cottage. I was trying to think why he'd be snooping around, but it didn't feel like something I could simply ask Mum, or tell her. She had enough going on, plus I doubt she'd have seen it the way I did. She'd have waved it away as something innocent. But Daniel knew Mum was still at dinner, so it felt like something he'd done on purpose.

Either way, I found myself inside and scrolling through my phone. I knew I was going to have to be up and invested in looking after the twins, but it had been such a long couple of days that I wasn't in the right frame of mind.

I checked the time and, even with the difference, I knew Tina would have just shut up the shop back at home.

Tina (friend of Emma McGinley): I was driving home but pulled over as soon as I saw that Emma was calling.

Emma: I work in Tina's clothes shop. After I was released, I thought the only job I could get would be with Dad – and that was if he'd have me. It would have meant working with him and, more importantly, Daniel, every day. It would never have lasted and I would have ended up breaking my probation. It was Tina who saved me.

Tina: I wouldn't go that far.

Emma: When my husband had divorced me and everyone else thought I was a monster, Tina was the one who said I could come and work with her. I'd have done it for free, but she set up a proper schedule where I'd get paid more after a certain length of time, or if I was opening up, that sort of thing. On the first day, she gave me a key for the shop and it meant so much that she trusted me. I was holding this little door key and I wanted to cry. I was pinching my thumb, trying to stop myself because it was such a silly thing.

Then she started encouraging me to go to these trade fairs where people buy vintage clothes in bulk. She said I had a better eye than her and that…

…

Sorry, I need a minute.

Julius: They should have come out as a couple. It's ridiculous. Everyone knows anyway.

Emma: We're not a couple. It's not like that. I can't believe someone would say that. She just… she means a lot to me.

Tina: Couple?! Ha! Who told you that? I think my girlfriend might have a thing or two to say about it.

Emma and I work together, that's all. Emma was going through a hard time and I've known her since we were kids. I offered her a chance and it turned out she's very good at what she does.

I know she says I saved her – but it's not true. She's the one who turned up on time every day. She's the one who loaded almost six-hundred pieces onto our website, all with photos. She's the one who bought two grand's worth of clothes in bulk and ended up selling everything individually for something like ten times that. All that was in the first six months she worked at the shop. If there was any saving to be done, then it was Emma who did it. She saved herself.

Emma: Tina saved me.

Julius: They were definitely a couple – if not now, then before the island.

Emma: We're in contact every day in some way or another. If it's during the week, we'll be in the shop together, unless we have a day off. Even when we're not in, we message through the day. I think I needed to hear Tina's voice.

Tina: I instantly knew something was wrong.

Emma: As soon as I started talking, Tina stopped me and asked what was wrong.

Tina: She was really cheery, which was a sign in itself. She was telling me how the flight was great and that the hotel was terrific. All that. I know Emma well enough to realise when something's up. I cut her off and asked what was really going on.

Emma: I said Dad had fallen off a cliff and that he was in a coma in the hospital.

Tina: She was in a bit of a state because her dad was in the hospital. I don't think I realised how serious it was at that point. She said everyone was due to be flying back at the end of the week, but her mum was likely going to have to remain with him for as long as was needed. Emma didn't want her mum to be by herself, so she said she might have to hang around for a little longer.

Emma: It hadn't really hit me until then. Julius had the girls, so he'd be going home. Liz and Daniel weren't going to stay – and I don't know why Victor and Claire were there in the first place. Unless I was going to leave Mum alone, it was going to have to be me who remained.

Tina: I told Emma not to worry about the shop; that she should take as long as she needed. I don't think that was necessarily what she wanted to hear because there was a long pause.

Emma: I don't remember everything I said.

Tina: Every time anyone goes on holiday, I think they have a secret hope that their workplace is going to fall to pieces without them. We all want to believe we're the most important part in any machine but, with Emma… perhaps she needed to be told that a bit more than other people. If I'd been through what she has, I think I'd be the same.

I asked if I could send some photos of jackets to her email so that she could tell me what she thought. She was so happy that I asked if she could upload the three she liked the most onto the website. She's got a logon, so could access it anywhere. I was assuming she'd taken her laptop.

It's what she wanted to hear, so it's what I told her.

Emma: It was good to hear Tina tell me about how the day had gone. There was a woman who wanted to try everything on and then ended up buying nothing. Someone else was going to a 60s-themed party but refused to believe all the things she liked were from a different decade. It sounded like fun.

Tina: It was just another day at work. I closed early because we were quiet.

Emma: I told her I was babysitting Chloe and Amy that night.

Tina: Her mood definitely changed across that phone call. I was surprised that she was going to be looking after the twins. I think I might have said 'By yourself?'

Emma: She told me I'd do great.

Tina: The biggest concern I had wasn't anything to do with Emma. If I had a child, I'd have no problem letting Emma look after him or her. It's not like she's a danger to children, or even that her judgement should be questioned. Not now, anyway.

My biggest worry was that Julius might be setting her up to fail. If something *did* go wrong when the girls were in Emma's care, then it would have been a lot for her to come back from. I only thought that because the relationship she has with her brother is… *complex.*

Emma: 'You'll do great' were her exact words. I think I needed the pep talk.

Tina: I wouldn't say they hated each other, certainly not then – but everything is complicated with Emma and her relationships. Things are bound to be when you've been through what she has. Things were difficult with her and her dad and probably the same with her brother. I wasn't sure that Julius had her best interests at heart. Actually, I wasn't sure that he had anyone's best interests at heart, other than his own. He has this way of saying the right things, even though he'll turn around and do the opposite.

I don't mind being wrong. I hoped I was. I remember telling Emma to be careful, but I wouldn't have said it like that. I'd have said something like: 'You're going to do great – but make sure you're careful.' I could hardly tell her to beware of her brother.

...

I don't think I've explained that very well. You'd have to know Emma and Julius to understand. You'd have to see them together. It's got to be hard when you know your older brother is the favourite child and always will be. If you're second-best among your own parents, then what sort of message does that give you when you're growing up? People think Emma's some spoiled rich girl who threw it all away, but you wouldn't say that if you knew her.

Emma: I think that was all Tina said.

Tina: I remember telling Emma that I hoped she was OK and that it was great to hear from her. I really meant that...

I hope I haven't sounded insincere here. I know how it might have come across, but I find it so difficult to talk about Emma. Sometimes I overanalyse the things we talk about, or her reaction to things.

I suppose I just want her to be happy. That makes sense, doesn't it? She's the best person I know, but she has a really good way of hiding it.

CHAPTER TEN

THE UNICORN HEAD

Emma: It was Chloe who answered the hotel room door when I knocked… or at least she *said* it was Chloe. The girls were wearing identical pink pyjamas and had tied their hair into these topknot ponytails. It was really hard to know for certain who was who.

Julius: Emma was running late, but I didn't want to ask what was going on. I was trusting her that she hadn't been drinking, or anything like that. I suppose there was a second where I thought leaving her to look after the girls might not be the best thing – but we're still family, aren't we? I wanted her to prove herself.

Emma: Julius left more or less straight away and I suddenly realised this was the first time I'd been alone with a child since before prison. It would have been about three years at that point, maybe a little less. I try not to think about it, but it never leaves you…

…

I wouldn't want it to.

Amy: I liked having Auntie Emma there. She wasn't always telling us to put things away, or to keep quiet.

Emma: Julius said that the girls were eager for me to be spending time with them, but they both seemed quite happy to be playing on their iPads. I had a thought that it wasn't like that when I was young – but I guess everyone feels like that. It used to be pop music, then TV, then video games. There's always something. When I was a girl, I would have been watching music videos on TV all day.

Chloe: She asked us what we thought of the hotel.

Emma: I was happy to sit with them while they played their games, but I remember that, when I was young, I always liked it when people asked me for my opinion. Adults don't always do that. You might go out for a family meal and someone always asks the grown-ups what they think of the place, or the food, or the price. The kids never get asked – or, if they do, it's in a sort of babyish, condescending way.

So I asked them what they thought of the hotel. I didn't think they'd heard me at first and then they both lowered their iPads at the same time. It was almost as if they'd planned it – although I don't think they had. Sometimes they do things in unison and it takes a moment to realise they've done it. It's like your eyes don't believe that something can be happening with such symmetry.

Chloe: I said it was nice – but not as nice as the Center Parcs that Mummy had taken us to at Easter.

Amy: Center Parcs is lush.

Chloe: It's really lush.

Emma: They brought up Simone, not me. She was my sister-in-law, but we were never really friends away from when we were in the family group. At that point, it would have been three to three-and-a-half years since we'd last spoken.

Amy: Dad said that, when we were with him, it was his time. When it was *Mum*'s time, we could talk about her as much as we liked.

Emma: They asked if I thought Julius and Simone would get back together. I didn't know what to say, so told them that it was a question they'd have to ask their dad when he got back.

The truth is that I can't see any way they'd ever get back together. Julius told everyone that Simone had been having an affair with her spinning teacher – and that she'd gone off with him. It's not that I necessarily thought that was untrue, more that there was probably more to it. Julius could be like that sometimes. He'd tell the truth – but only a half-truth.

When we were kids, Julius once told Dad a boy had been picking on him, so he'd turned around and knocked the lad to the ground. Maybe it was a generational thing, but Dad liked to hear things like that.

It was true... except that the boy was only picking on Julius because Julius had been bullying that boy's younger sister. Then Julius *had* knocked the lad to the ground – but only because he'd run at him from behind and hit him with a rock. He didn't lie to Dad – but it wasn't the whole story.

I thought that's probably what he was doing when he used to tell the family stories about Simone.

When it comes to things like divorces or separation, it's rare that the blame is all on one side...

...

Except with my divorce, of course. That was nobody's fault but mine.

Extract of a letter received from Tite, Tite and Gaze Solicitors, on behalf of Simone McGinley: My client would like to point out that the document agreed to between her and Mr Julius McGinley cited *his* 'unreasonable behaviour' as grounds for divorce. There was no need for any further notations in the agreement. That is a fact which speaks for itself.

Emma: Chloe said that her mum doesn't cry as much any more. It was really direct, in the way kids can be sometimes. I didn't know how to reply, so I probably said something like: 'Oh, that's good.'

Luckily they moved on, because they wanted to know what had happened to their granddad.

Chloe: Dad wouldn't tell us anything.

Emma: I asked what Julius had told them. They said he'd let on that their granddad had fallen down and had to go to hospital. I didn't want to lie to them, but it wasn't like I could bypass their dad and tell them everything. They were only eight and I didn't want them to have nightmares about cliffs and falling. I told them that Granddad had fallen over and that he was recovering.

Chloe: I liked talking to Auntie Emma. She didn't say that she wanted to watch the telly instead.

Emma: The girls would drift from one subject to the next, even though one thing might have nothing in common with one another. It was like they'd built up this big folder of questions over a period of time. Because I was doing my best to answer, they decided to throw everything at me.

They asked about electric cars, because one of their neighbours had recently got one. They wanted to know what happened after you separated all the plastic for recycling. They thought it was hilarious that their granddad still bought a newspaper. I didn't understand why at first – and then they said that you could read everything on an iPad. It was that different way of seeing the world.

We must have talked for about an hour, more or less non-stop. I don't remember everything – but there was definitely a moment where they asked what was wrong with their dad. I didn't know what they meant at first. I think it was Amy who said that he kept holding onto his side and that he would do some breathing exercises each morning. I was a bit blank at first – but then I remembered he'd winced when he was at the shop counter outside the airport.

I told them that when people get older, bits of their bodies can start to wear out. Then they started talking about how they'd get robot body parts if any of theirs wore out.

Amy: Auntie Emma said I can have robot legs that will help me run really fast.

Emma: It was inevitable where things were going to lead. They had probably been asking their parents for a year or two about it. In the end, I think it was Chloe who asked what prison was like.

Chloe: Daddy told us never to ask Auntie Emma about prison…

Emma: I didn't want to give them nightmares – but I didn't want to be evasive. When I was released, it was one of the things I decided I would do for the rest of my life. I wouldn't bring up what happened unless I had to – but I wouldn't lie about it, either. If people had questions, then I'd answer them.

So I told the girls that prison wasn't very nice and that nobody should ever want to go.

Amy: Unca Daniel said people poo in a bucket in prison.

Chloe: He said there's a bucket in every prison room and that people have to poo in it. Then they sleep in the room with the poo and the poo goes everywhere.

Emma: At some point, they must have asked 'Unca' Daniel about prison. I don't know where or when that would have happened – but he told them something about buckets and going to the toilet. You know what it's like when kids hear a rude-ish word and then can't stop saying it… They asked if I slept in a poopy room and if I could smell the poo. How are you supposed to reply? I told them prison wasn't like that, but they were giggling so much, I don't think it mattered. It took them about fifteen minutes to calm down. Every time it quietened a little, one of them would whisper 'poo' – and they'd be off again.

Daniel: I tried to scare them straight. Haven't you ever heard of that? If I make you think prison is a scary place, you won't want to go, will you? It's basic logic. You can hardly tell them it's all like a holiday camp nowadays.

Amy: Unca Daniel said prison's like a holiday camp nowadays.
   Chloe: I didn't know what a holiday camp was… but I like holidays… like Center Parcs.

Emma: I soon realised why they had so many questions. Daniel had told them that prison is a 'holiday camp'. When they said they didn't know what a holiday camp was, he said prisons were 'better than Butlin's' – but they didn't know what Butlin's was, either.
   I can imagine him getting frustrated at that point, so he told them that all prisoners had their own television and a PlayStation. That being sent to prison was like being sent on holiday. That obviously made them say that they quite liked the sound of prison – which is why he told them that everyone poos in a bucket.

...
Imagine telling all that to a pair of eight-year-old girls.

Daniel: I said no such thing.

Amy: ...
   ...
   ...
   Poo.

Emma: We ended up playing a card game. They had played Uno before and had some Old Maid cards back at home – but they really liked the idea of me teaching them a game with actual cards. The only thing I could think of was Shithead, but I obviously couldn't tell them that was the name, so I called it Unicorn Head.

Chloe: We play Unicorn Head all the time now.

Emma: We played until the girls could barely keep their eyes open. They said they wanted to keep going but didn't protest too much when I put them to bed. I'd planned to read them a story, but they were both asleep as soon as their heads hit the pillows.

I stood and watched them for a little bit... not long... but it was comforting to see them like that. They were so slim and small... so precious. They were taking these long, deep breaths and it left me feeling hopeful about the future.

It was true when I said that I sometimes found it hard to see them or be around them – but I think I got over it that night. I started to think that I could maybe babysit them as a regular thing. Julius only had the girls every other weekend, but I thought about contacting Simone and offering to look after the girls if she needed a hand.

   ...

It was a fantasy, of course. I don't think she'd have agreed and, even if she had, everything changed before we left the island.

…

Whatever happened later, I have to thank Julius for giving me those few hours. He didn't have to and I'll always have that evening. It might sound odd to say, but it was one of the best nights of my life.

Amy: When we got home, Daddy told us Auntie Emma is a bad person who does bad things.

Chloe: He said that bad people sometimes act like good people – but that they're still bad people.

Emma: After the girls fell asleep, I went out onto the balcony to get a bit of air. Galanikos can be stifling in the evenings sometimes. The heat of the day doesn't clear and everything feels so close that you're desperate to get away from it. That night, though, it was so much crisper and fresher than it had been earlier. It felt like the island was resetting itself. There was a chill on my skin and I wished it was always like that.

The balcony overlooks the bar and there were still quite a lot of people out. I was sitting and watching. It was the usual holiday thing. Some people were dancing badly, while others were lining up shots across the bar. I spotted Victor and Claire standing near a piano. They were close to each other but angled away. I didn't notice it right away – but then I realised they were having some sort of conversation, even though they weren't facing one another. Their lips would move and then the other's body would stand more rigidly.

I think they were probably arguing, although I don't know for sure. It was more the way they were going out of their way to not look at each other.

Claire: We argued more or less non-stop on the island.

Emma: I couldn't hear anything over the music – but out of nowhere, Claire suddenly spun and then marched away. I think Victor called after her, but she ignored him and kept going. I watched him and he watched her. He didn't move for a good thirty seconds after she'd gone, as if he couldn't believe it. There was something about the way he was holding himself in, that time. The way his head was arched forward, with his shoulders tight and tense. I probably knew what was going to happen – and then it did.

Claire: I was back in the hotel by then. I only know what people said the next day.

Emma: There was a man who was on his way to the bar. He was going past Victor and they touched shoulders. He turned back to say sorry – but Victor swung at him before the guy knew what was happening. The punch landed somewhere on the man's chin or cheek – and he toppled backwards into the piano. There was this enormous bang and the sound of tinkling keys.

I thought Victor might turn and run, but he did the opposite. Even though the other man was on the floor, Victor launched himself at him and started swinging his fists back and forth. It was one punch after another – maybe five or six – until a couple of blokes pulled him off. I couldn't hear the words, but he was shouting and raging, still trying to fight even though there were three people holding him back.

There was a time when violence would shock me, but, on that night, I realised how much I'd changed. How desensitised I was. I didn't want to be that person, but it's like Pandora's Box, isn't it? When something's out, it can't be put back.

Five or six security guards showed up then and pulled Victor away. They pinned his arms behind his back and one of them had him by the neck. Victor was still trying to get away but had no chance. They dragged him out through a side door and there was a moment of calm confusion in the bar, where everyone stopped and looked to everyone else, wondering what had just happened.

It was only a second, maybe two, where there was this eerie, confusing peace. Like when you've been running a bath and then you turn off the taps and there's a final drip before the silence.

Then it started to rain.

CHAPTER ELEVEN

DAY THREE

THE SHEPHERD AND SAILOR

Emma: I didn't sleep a lot that night… I'm not sure how anyone could have. Julius got back to the room not long after Victor was taken away. The twins were still sleeping – I don't think they'd moved – and then I headed off to the cottage.

The thunder and lightning started about half an hour after the rain, and it went through most of the night. Every time it felt like things were quietening down, there would be another boom of thunder and then the rain would clatter on the roof louder than before. I thought about checking on Mum, but I didn't want to wake her in case she was sleeping through it.

Claire: I didn't know there had been a storm until the next day. I've always been a heavy sleeper.

Julius: I don't know what Emma did with the girls, but they didn't stir all night. I slept here and there, but, every time I dropped off, the thunder came back.

Daniel: Slept like a log.

Emma: It was around four in the morning when I went onto the little patio at the side of the cottage. There was a big umbrella next to an outdoor table and I sat under that watching the lightning hit the ocean. The thunder would boom at almost the same moment as the light and there was something so… *primal* about it all.

I enjoyed it.

Julius: I watched the end of the storm from the balcony. There were quite a few lights on from the other windows of the hotel and I think lots of people were doing the same. I thought about getting the girls up, but they were sleeping so peacefully. I can't remember the last time they were that tired.

Emma: There was a coffee machine in the cottage, so I made myself a mug and then watched the storm peter out. It was only a little while later that the sun started to rise. The view from the hotel is nowhere near as wide or clear as the one from the cliffs – but I sat and watched it anyway. The sky was flaming orange and I thought about the old saying 'Red sky in the morning, shepherd's warning.'

Claire: Red sky in the morning, sailor's warning.

Emma: Some of the staff were sweeping water into the drains, but, within about an hour, it was as if the storm had never happened. Everything was dry again and the sky was cloudless and blue. I thought about Dad in hospital and wondered if there would be more improvement. I thought about Mum and her diagnosis – plus how this was the last thing she needed. The holiday felt like a mistake, but I'd had such a great night with the twins that I was stuck not knowing how I really thought about it.

Julius: I pulled the curtains and went back to bed as soon as the lightning stopped.

Emma: Before prison, I never understood exercise. I hated PE at school and didn't see how anyone could ever take pleasure from running around.

When I was inside, it was a gradual thing, but gym became the thing I looked forward to the most. It became the start of my routine before I knew that could be so important.

That morning, after the storm, my legs were itching, like they were craving the exercise I'd not given them in a couple of days. I went into the cottage and put on my running gear and then left the hotel.

If I'd waited another couple of hours, it would have been too hot, but the temperature was perfect.

I ran down the slope towards the village just as a pair of delivery trucks were pulling in. There was one with a Coca-Cola logo and another with Pepsi. It was this really normal thing and yet you'd never see it during the day. There was a peacefulness about something so utterly mundane.

I continued through the village and out the other side. The road gets narrower there and the verges are overgrown grass. It was only as I was running past it that I remembered the Grand Paradise Hotel. They'd started building it ten years before and, at the time, it was said that it was going to be the biggest and best on the island. There were brochures and Dad had talked about switching our annual booking to the new hotel when it was ready.

When I ran past the site, I realised that it was still this half-finished, abandoned patch of land. I didn't stop running, but I did slow and look across the site. There were foundations and a couple of walls – but that was about it. I suppose the developer ran out of money. The grass was up above my knees and it didn't look as if anyone had worked there in a very long time.

I kept moving and cut in on a path that took me out towards the cliffs. I stayed away from the edge but followed the shape of the ridge all the way back around the coast until I ended up going past that single cone that was still on the spot where Dad fell.

It was laughable really. Worse than having nothing there.

After that, I was back at the front of the hotel. I was sweating so much that it was running into my eyes and stinging. Trying to rub it away was only making it worse, which is why I almost missed Mum walking towards the taxi. I was past her when she called my name. I stopped and tried to clear my eyes while she asked what I was doing. I didn't get a chance to answer before she laughed and said it was a stupid question. She told me she was off to the hospital, but then asked if I was going back to the cottages. She said she'd forgotten her phone charger and that she wanted to take it to the hospital in case she ended up being there all day.

I've thought of that moment quite a bit since it happened – but I honestly can't remember whether she asked me to fetch it for her. I think it might have been one of those things that was implied. If she was going back for her charger, she would have said that.

Whatever was said, I ended up going through the hotel, out towards the cottages.

I went into mine first to grab a towel – and then let myself into Mum's with the spare key I'd been given by the manager. Mum hadn't told me where the charger was, but I started by looking next to her bed, because that's where I keep mine. The first thing I noticed was that the bed didn't look slept in… either that, or Mum had got up and made the bed herself. It was probably nothing important – but I forgot to ask her about it because of what happened next.

I couldn't see her charger in the bedroom, so I went through to the combined living room and kitchen area. There was a big suitcase on a table that was resting in an alcove of the wall. I thought the charger might be in there, so opened it up and started looking.

…

I didn't go looking for that envelope – it was just there, sand-wiched between a pair of Dad's trousers. The flap wasn't sealed. Maybe I opened it up to see what was inside, or maybe it fell out. I don't think it matters. I don't know why anyone would care how I found it, only about what was inside.

I should have taken a photo of it so that people would believe me later on, but that's easy to say after the event. At the time, I was struggling to understand what it meant. I almost didn't believe what I was seeing. I picked it up and turned it over, then twisted it around, trying to convince myself it was real.

It was a driving licence: a normal, British plastic card with Dad's photo on it. He was giving one of those dead-eye stares to the camera like you have to do for those things. You're not allowed to look human – but anyone would still recognise their own dad.

The problem was that it wasn't Dad's name on that licence – it was Alan's.

CHAPTER TWELVE

THE BEST PASTRIES

Emma: I couldn't figure it out. I wondered if it was an old licence that actually belonged to Alan – but the issue date was from about six months earlier. By that point, Alan had already been dead for more than eight years. Then there was Dad's photo. Everything looked new.

When I was fifteen, one of my friends at school said she could get us all fake IDs. There were about ten of us and we all gave her a fiver with a passport photo. She came back after the weekend with an envelope full of fake student cards, with every one making us seem three years older than we were. I had my first drink in a pub using that card. I was thinking of that as I was holding the envelope. It was a fake ID, with Dad's photo and Alan's details.

When we were kids, we needed those cards to make us look older – but Dad had this to make him look like Alan… to make him look like a man who'd died nine years before…

It wasn't just the ID in the envelope. There were a couple of sheets of paper and a small key. I remember 'Ag Georgios' being written across the top and thought it was probably a person. There was a separate line that had '#133' on it.

I definitely glanced at the rest but didn't pay much attention because I was supposed to be finding Mum's charger. I ended up stuffing everything into the envelope and putting it back where it came from.

It was only then that I saw Mum's charger on the ledge next to the front door. She'd probably put it down on her way out and forgotten to pick it up. I grabbed that and then opened the door… but I couldn't leave that envelope where it was. I just couldn't. I ended up locking it in my cottage before running back to the taxi with Mum's charger. I thought she might say something about the length of time I took, but she simply said 'thank you' – and then she left.

It didn't even cross my mind to mention the fake ID to her then. Maybe I should have?

All I can say is that you weren't there. People always read books or watch movies and judge the main character as if it's them. They say 'No one would ever act like that!' – but what they're really saying is that *they* wouldn't. Except it's not their story and it's not their circumstances. They haven't lived a whole life in someone else's shoes. What those people are really saying isn't that 'no one would ever act like that', it's: 'My existence and my thought patterns are so ingrained that I can't imagine anyone acting in a way differently to me.'

You have to have a real ego to think like that.

Julius: It was quite a bit later when I heard what Emma claimed about that licence. I don't know what to say about it. Either it existed and she was wrong about the details – or she made the whole thing up. Ask yourself this: If she'd found what she said she did, then where is it? She didn't take a photo, she didn't show anyone, she didn't ask Mum about it.

If it was me, I'd have done all those things. Wouldn't you?

Emma: After Mum's taxi left, I was heading back through reception. There was a woman there talking to a man behind the counter. She wasn't shouting, but she was speaking loudly enough that anyone could hear what she was saying. She was at that point where you're not sure if you're upset, angry, or both. Where your voice is wavering as you're trying to hold yourself together.

The guy behind the counter was trying to make a phone call as she was telling him how someone had been in her room and stolen cash. It was the specifics that stuck with me. She wasn't just saying 'money', she was saying 'three hundred and sixty euros' over and over.

If she'd not been there, I don't think I'd have noticed the map next to the main desk. I glanced across towards her and spotted a large picture of the island on the wall. I don't remember it being there when we arrived, but I guess I wasn't paying attention.

I went over to it and stared. It was taller than me, with the entire outline of Galanikos, with the roads and the villages. I don't think I'd ever looked at the island like that before. I'd always thought of it as this one village with the hotels and the market – but there were other villages, too. A road ran from the south-west corner all along the bottom of the island and then up to the north-east before stopping when it got to the mountain that's up there. There were intermittent markers the whole way around – and that's when I saw the dot that read 'Agios Georgios' over to the east.

Extract from official guide to Galanikos: The largest village on the island of Galanikos is also named Galanikos, although it is colloquially known as 'The Village'. The extinct volcano that created the island – and which dominates the north-west corner – is *also* called Galanikos. Other villages on the island include Ermones, Vatos, Agios Georgios (Saint George) and Kokkini.

Emma: A member of staff must have noticed me next to the map because she came over and asked if there was anything I was looking for. I asked her about 'Agios Georgios' and she immediately said 'Saint George'. She seemed a bit confused about why I was interested, so I asked her what was there. She gave this sort of shrug like you do when you're not sure what to say. I thought it might be a language issue, but it wasn't at all. She goes: 'No tourists.' I misunderstood and replied: 'Tourists aren't allowed?' She laughed and then said: 'No reason for tourists to go. There's nothing there.'

I didn't get it at first, but then I realised it would be like running into a tourist on their way into Britain. You'd think they were visiting London or Edinburgh – but then they point to somewhere like Grimsby and you'd think, 'Why are you going *there*?' She couldn't get her head around it.

I asked her if there was a bus that went there and she couldn't stop herself from laughing. She said there was one bus in the morning and one that went later, with nothing during the day. Other than that, anyone could drive.

Someone called her away and she walked off still saying 'Agios Georgios' under her breath as if I'd just told her an amazing joke.

Claire: I don't know what Emma said to the woman in reception, but she found it hilarious. I think she went off to tell her co-worker about it.

Emma: I was about to go back to the cottage when I noticed Claire was standing almost right behind me. It was only then I remembered Victor being dragged off after he punched that guy. Claire had this half grin on her face and she goes…

Claire: 'How was your night?'

Emma: I didn't know if she was joking. It *felt* like she was.

Claire: I can't remember any more. I told her the manager had been to my room and said that Victor was being held in the police cells for punching a guy in the hotel last night. It was all news to me. We'd had an argument and then I'd gone to bed. He hadn't come back to the room, but let's say it wouldn't have been the first time Victor stayed out all night.

Emma: I told her I saw what happened because I was on Julius's balcony. She didn't seem surprised that he'd punched a guy unprovoked.

Claire: Is there an opposite of surprised? Unsurprised? Predictable? Par for the course? That was me when Emma said it was unprovoked.

Emma: I asked her if she was going to the cells and Claire snorted.

Claire: Oh, I remember what I said. I looked her right in the eye, shook my head, and said: 'Let him rot.'

Then I went to the breakfast buffet. Best pastries I've ever had.

CHAPTER THIRTEEN

THE COMPLICATED EMOTIONS THERE

Emma: It was early and hardly anyone was up. I would have still been in my running gear at that point, probably still sweating from the run. I went back to the cottage for a shower and then grabbed that envelope with the driving licence inside. I wanted to act before anyone had a chance to do anything – or, more likely, before I had a chance to talk or think myself out of it.

I still had that business card I'd been given at the pool, so went to the car hire place where the same man who'd given me the card was setting up. He greeted me like an old friend, even though that moment by the pool was the only time we'd met. He told me he was called Barak and I don't mind admitting I was nervous about being there. It's a long time since I've been anything other than a passenger in a car and that's why I felt a twinge of relief as I spotted the problem.

The guy offering cheap car hire was standing in front of a small but clearly empty car park. He said the cards had been more popular than he'd expected, which I guess was self-evident. He told me there would be cars returning late morning, or in the afternoon, and that he'd save the best one for me. I probably rolled my eyes in the way you do when someone's calling you 'pretty lady' and making promises. I said I'd go back later and turned to go.

That's when I saw Scott for the first time in nine years.

Scott Lee (Son of Alan Lee, former business partner of Geoffrey McGinley): We saw each other at the same time. Emma had been talking to the guy at the car hire place and turned around just as I was walking past.

I'd not seen her in nine years, but I recognised her straight away. I don't think it was the obvious stuff, like her hair colour or anything like that; it was the way she stood. There was a time when we were really close and, when you're like that, you know everything about a person. You can tell who they are from streets away. You know who they are from behind. Their shadow, their gait, the shape of their hands, the way they tilt their head. It's not like you actively think about any of those things, it's that they become intrinsic. You just know – and I knew Emma the moment I saw her.

Emma: There's one very important thing you need to know about Scott and his thinking at this point.

Scott: Her dad killed my dad.

Emma: It wasn't just that he thought my dad killed his, it's that he was driven by it.

Scott: I wouldn't use the word 'driven'. It makes it sound worse than it was. I didn't stay up all night with a map of the resort and a length of string, while trying to measure distances and comparing them to the angle of a sunset. I had a normal job and a normal life. I went to the football on a weekend and did a big shop every Monday night. Life was very normal... it's just that Geoff McGinley killed my dad and I wasn't prepared to forget it.

Emma: I didn't know what to say. It was enough that *I* was back on the island – but he was there, too. A big reunion that none of us planned or wanted.

It felt like a whole bunch of thoughts were rushing at me all together. It was less than an hour ago that I'd seen *his* dad's name on that driving licence with *my* dad's photo. Then there was one burning thought I couldn't get rid of.

Scott pushed my dad off the cliff.

Scott: I didn't push her dad off the cliff.

Emma: No one had a better motive. Scott had spent nine years believing my dad killed his and then, suddenly, he's up on the cliffs and he sees that man standing on the edge. It was so clear in my mind that it was as if I was watching it happen.

Scott: I was nowhere near those cliffs when her dad fell.

Emma: I was so focused on Scott that I didn't even notice who was walking directly behind him.

Paul: I think I probably waved at Emma, although I'd have been trying to play it cool because I wouldn't have wanted the rest of the team to see. We had that great night together and then I'd not heard from her the whole of the next day. It's not like we swapped numbers, or made promises – but I'd been keeping an eye out for her around the hotel and village, hoping I'd see her.

Then, all of a sudden, there she was.

Emma: I knew Paul was making a documentary about Alan, but I didn't realise that documentary actually involved Scott being on the island. Worlds were colliding.

Paul: We were doing a bit of prep for that day's filming. Scott was walking us through the village first thing in the morning before it got too busy. We'd got a few minutes of framing shots that could be spliced in for creating a mood, plus I'd gone to the beach and recorded the sound of the waves crashing. We didn't know if we'd need it, but it was there.

Emma: It wasn't just Scott at the front, with Paul behind. There were four of you there and—

Sorry, I said 'you'. Is that OK?

AUTHOR'S NOTE

This seems like a good time to explain that *After the Accident* began life as a documentary about the death of Alan Lee on the island of Galanikos.

There's an old journalistic saying that the reporter should never be the subject of their piece. I agree wholeheartedly with this, except that, as the team from Garibaldi Media visited the island to start shooting, a larger story overtook the one on which they were working.

The story of the two falls have to be told together. Like it or not, Alan and Geoff are linked.

In addition, there would also be an enormous narrative gap without including Paul and Scott. That is why some of the transcripts you have been reading come from interviews done on the island, while others had to take place at a later date.

Emma: It wasn't just Scott at the front, with Paul behind. There were four men there. Paul was carrying a boom mic over his shoulder and the guy behind him had a large pack on his shoulders. He looked like he was doing most of the work. The one at the back seemed to be ordering everyone around. He had a big mouth and a fat arse and a stupid walk and—

OK, he didn't have any of those things. The truth is, I didn't really notice the guy at the back because I was so stunned by both Paul and Scott being there.

Paul: When we first met, Emma laughed at me for goldfishing – but she was much worse. Then Scott said her name.

Scott: I'd stopped, which meant the guys had also stopped. It seemed stupid to pretend we didn't know each other. At first I thought Emma was trying to avoid looking at me. It was much later when I found out she already knew Paul.

Emma: I was staring at Paul, trying to tell him with my eyes that I was sorry. He was looking between Scott and me, probably putting the pieces together.

Paul: I can't remember how I felt at the time. Probably confused.

Emma: It was like a blink and I was in front of Scott. I'd somehow crossed the path without knowing I'd done it.

We used to be friends in the way people are when they grow up together. Our dads owned a business together, so we'd end up being left alone to play while the grown-ups talked downstairs. We'd always be at each other's houses, or told to go out and amuse ourselves. Julius was older than me and used to say that Scott was my boyfriend – but we were much too young for that.

By the time we became teenagers, we drifted apart. I had my friends at school and he had his. We didn't need to be together all the time when our parents were working because we had our own hobbies and interests.

Scott: Is that what she said? It's... well it's sort of true. We definitely went our own way as teenagers, but that's because she dropped me. She was in with all the popular kids.

I had quite bad acne when I was that age. I had to have this special cream from the pharmacy and it reeked. Dad made me sit in my room with my door closed and the windows open. It used to make me gag.

Emma: Acne? I don't remember that. We were teenagers: we all had acne. Me and my group of friends were like a walking Clearasil advert. If you're a teenager who stops being friends with people because they have spots, you're going to be a very lonely person.

Scott: I understand why it happened like it did. She had money because of her dad, plus she was pretty and her chest had exploded when she hit about fourteen.

Yeah, I noticed that. I was a teenage boy. We tend to pay close attention to that sort of thing.

Emma was everything I wasn't and she didn't want to hang around with me, so we stopped being friends around then. We'd still see each other because of our dads, but it was never the same. We could go months without talking – and then it was years. The only time I ever saw her was if we all ended up on Galanikos together.

Emma: ...

　　...

I don't think any of it is quite as brutal as he makes it sound. It's not like I woke up one day and thought, 'He's not my friend any more'. Things happen gradually. We'd be in different classes and I'd have a lot in common with the person I was sitting next to. We might go straight from that class to the canteen, so I'd eat with the person I was already hanging around with. I didn't try to cut out Scott from my life, but the two of us were changing.

...

I don't know if I should bring this up – but he started talking to my chest and not my face. He'd do it *all* the time. I know that he was fourteen or fifteen, that there's hormones and all that, but why would I want to be friends with someone who looks at me like that? That's what I mean when I say the *two* of us were changing.

Scott: Maybe this isn't the place to say it, but you've probably guessed. Emma was my first love. I doubt I was hers, but it's like that when you're a kid. She was a girl I'd grown up with and then, suddenly, she was a woman.

I'd have these long, ridiculous fantasy conversations with her where I'd say something, and then she'd say something, and then we'd realise we were meant to be together...

I was probably sixteen then, but you don't know how anything works at that age. Your body is desperately trying to get you to be an adult, while your mind is stuck watching *Ninja Turtles* on a Saturday morning.

That probably lasted for about three years in all. I think the first time I finally stopped thinking about Emma like that was when I got to uni and met a girl during freshers' week.

Emma: Did he really say I was his first love?

...

I kind of want to give him a hug and say sorry. First loves never go right, do they? I never felt like that about him, but I do wish we'd been better friends.

First love? That poor guy.

Scott: Bear in mind, when I saw Emma outside that car hire place, not only do I know that her dad killed my dad, I still have all those old teenage thoughts going through my head. I've not seen her properly in nine years and there's a lot of complicated emotions there.

Emma: Scott turned to the crew and goes: 'This is Emma. Her dad killed mine. Put that in your film.'

Scott: I probably shouldn't have said that.

Emma: By this point, everyone is looking at me. I'm still trying to tell Paul I'm sorry without actually telling him. But I'm also thinking of the driving licence I found that morning and wondering for the first time if, maybe, my dad *does* know something about what happened with Alan…

Perhaps I don't mean it quite like that. I had a lot of questions and hardly any answers.

Paul: I thought I was going to compromise the entire project. There were only three of us on the crew and we'd made the expense of going to the island – then I'd slept with the daughter of the man who might well have been prime suspect.

Emma: There was a long pause where nobody seemed to know what to say, then I go: 'Dad didn't kill anyone.'

Scott: When Dad died, the only person who benefitted was Geoff. With the way things worked out, he got sole charge of the company – and then he brought in someone new.

Emma: Scott was right about that – but so what? After Dad fell, I got to move into a beautiful cottage. *I* benefitted, but that doesn't mean I was involved.

That's how I thought about things at the time.

Scott: She went back to that old line of saying how the police cleared her dad, blah-blah-blah. I told her that the police found no evidence. It's not the same thing. What's indisputable is that her dad wasn't in his room at the time my dad went off that cliff.

Emma: That's true. Dad never denied that.

Paul: Things were tense and one of the crew said that we should move on. I had two points of view. My professional opinion was that, if we were going to have this conversation with Scott and Emma, then it should be on camera. My personal opinion was that I was in trouble.

Scott: I said something like 'see you around' and carried on walking.

Emma: He said: 'I don't know how you sleep at night'.

Paul: I started following everyone else and then stopped to tie my shoe. I told the rest of the crew I'd catch up but then went back to Emma.

Emma: I said 'sorry' straight away. I was mortified. I still think about it sometimes. I should have told him who I was on that first night and then, if things had happened after that, at least he knew.

Paul: It felt like a genuine apology. I think I laughed it off, saying 'We had a good time, didn't we?' Something like that. I still thought I might have endangered the whole project.

Emma: I asked where the crew were staying and how long they'd been there.

Paul: I didn't get what she meant at first. She already knew where I was staying, but she was really asking about Scott. I told her that he was in a villa a little along the road from the hotels. We'd all arrived about four hours before she did.

Emma: I was trying to figure out if Scott really had a chance to push Dad. His villa was around half a mile away from the cliff.

Paul: I asked her why she didn't tell me who she was. She knew what I was filming, so she must have realised the connection.

Emma: I told him I was having a good time and didn't want to spoil it.

Paul: Perhaps she was playing up to my ego with that. I don't know. The more you find out about Emma, the more complicated she is. When you read about what she did, it sounds like the worst thing in the world. Something that's the very definition of unforgiveable. You think that, if it was you, you'd never go outside again.

But then you see her, and you talk to her, and it makes you question everything. Life isn't black and white, with villains and heroes. Good people do awful things and awful people do good. I suppose the difficulty is in knowing the difference.

Friends who know what happened with Emma and me on the island have said that I'm crazy for believing her.

When she said she was having a good time with me and didn't want to spoil it… well… of course it was flattering. Of course I wanted to believe her. That doesn't mean she was manipulating me, or that it wasn't the truth.

Emma: I really *was* having a good time with him that night.

Paul: I told her I had to leave. A person can only stop to tie their shoes for so long and I didn't want any of the crew coming back to check on me. I'd probably taken a step or two away when I figured I'd try my luck.

Emma: He asked if I'd do an interview on camera to give the other side of Scott's story.

Paul: She didn't say 'no' – but she did say it probably wasn't a good idea. That's when I asked her if she fancied a drink instead.

Emma: Smooth, huh? I told him that would be a better idea. After that, he jogged away to catch up with the crew and Scott. I guess I watched him, trying to take in everything that had happened.

The village was starting to come alive by this time. The delivery trucks were back and stallholders were setting up. That hum of activity was beginning and the shadows were starting to stretch as the sun climbed higher.

Perhaps the strangest thing about that morning was the sheer level of inception going on. Scott was watching me talk to Barak, then, when Scott and I were talking, what neither of us realised was that we were being watched, too.

CHAPTER FOURTEEN

LANDER

Lander Contos (Resident of Galanikos): I was walking through the village and then, from nowhere, she was on the side of the road. We'd not seen one another in nine years, but I knew it was Emma the moment I saw her. I think it's something about the way she stands... the way she moves. It's like she has an assurance of who she is. I looked towards her and she'd changed but... not really.

I didn't think I'd ever see her again and then, suddenly, there she was.

Emma: When I'd been talking to Police Chief Jin on the cliffs, he'd mentioned Lander and then I'd sort of forgotten. It wasn't anything to do with Lander, it was more that so many other things had been going on.

Lander: There were four or five guys around her and I think, maybe, they were arguing. I was standing on the other side of the road, just watching. It didn't cross my mind to intervene. I think I was in shock.

Emma: After Paul walked off to catch up with his crew, I felt my neck prickling with that sense of being watched. I think I probably shivered – then I turned and saw Lander on the other side of the street. I suppose it was a morning for reintroductions.

Lander: She came across to where I was standing and we looked at each other for a few seconds. I couldn't think of what to say. There was probably a part of me that still couldn't believe she was actually there.

Emma: We were outside a tea shop and so I asked if he wanted one for old times.

Lander: I should have said no – but I don't think I've ever said no to Emma.

Emma: He snapped out of the trance he was in and ended up ordering for the pair of us. It's not like there's a huge menu in those island cafés. They do thick coffee, or something called Mountain Tea. It's made from leaves grown on the slopes of the volcano. Everybody from Galanikos drinks it and it's as common as tap water might be in Britain. I've never been much of a tea drinker back home, but Mountain Tea is something else. You have to try it to believe it.

Lander: I asked how she was.

Emma: I said I was good. There's a reflex in that answer. When you've not seen someone in nine years and they ask how you are, you don't immediately unload about how everything went badly wrong.

Lander: I told her I was good, too.

Emma: So there we were: both good.

I remember looking at his face and taking him in. His skin had always been this beautiful golden brown, but it had gone darker as the wrinkles were starting to come through around his eyes. His hairline had started to edge up his forehead a little and there was the merest whisper of grey close to his ears. I bet he's dyed it out by now.

Lander: I'm not going grey.

Emma: It made him look older, but I think it suited him. Some people grow out of their looks, but others grow into them.

It felt like another lifetime that we used to sneak off to the beach and cosy away in that cove underneath the cliffs. I never thought we'd end up as some old married couple… but I also didn't think we'd go almost a decade without seeing one another. There was this part of me that thought we'd always be in one another's lives, even though that made no sense.

Lander: She told me about her clothes shop, but I was confused by that. I said: 'Didn't you used to work for your dad?'

Emma: It wasn't the time to talk about that – and he wasn't the person to talk to.

Lander: She didn't want to talk about herself and kept asking questions about me instead.

Emma: He was married with two little girls. Who'd have guessed?

Lander: Do you want to see a picture? The girls look just like Rhea. Three beautiful women. I'm a lucky man.

Emma: His wife is called Rhea. I don't think he said it enough. Rhea, Rhea, Rhea. Did he mention his wife is called Rhea?

Lander: Emma said 'Oh' – but I didn't know what that meant. Was she surprised? Happy? Did she think I'd be waiting for her?

Emma: Of course I didn't want him to wait. That's ridiculous. I was surprised, that's all. I never really thought of Lander as the marrying type. Then he kept saying 'Rhea' over and over.

Lander: It was awkward.

Emma: It wasn't *that* awkward. I ended up pointing out towards the Grand Paradise and saying something about how they'd never finished the hotel.

Lander: We used to sneak away on the really hot days. They had almost finished building part of the lower floor for the new hotel, so there was a roof and shade.

...

She was trying to avoid the issue, so I said it outright.

Emma: 'You never came back.'

Lander: I said: 'You never came back.' She kind of looked away and I don't think she wanted to be there.

Emma: I tried to explain that, after everything with Alan's fall, my family didn't want to return. He didn't reply, but I understand what he was probably thinking. I never emailed or wrote. I didn't call or text…

I'm not a perfect person. I've never even claimed to be a *nice* person. I should have done things differently – but there wasn't much I could do nine years on.

Lander: She told me they were back for her parents' anniversary and her mum's birthday. She said her mum was ill and that this might be her last holiday. Then she said that her dad had fallen two nights before.

It was one thing after another, no time to take anything in and then—

Emma: Then I met Rhea.

Lander: I love my wife very much.

Emma: You know when you're walking along the street and you feel that awful squelch? You probably smell it before you see it and then you look back and realise you've just stepped in a dog poo?

That's more or less how Rhea looked at me.

Lander: Rhea is a very passionate woman.

Emma: On an island like Galanikos, the local lads and the white girls only tend to know each other for one reason.

As soon as Lander saw Rhea, he shot up as if he'd been electrocuted. He said: 'This is Emma. We used to be friends.' He might as well have said nothing because Rhea knew right away who I was.

Lander: I had forgotten that I had work to do.

Emma: I don't think she actually said anything. She might have coughed, or perhaps she just stood there. He mumbled something like 'goodbye' – and then the two of them hurried off along the road.

They were almost out of sight when Rhea turned back to look at me. You know that saying about how looks can kill? She could have committed genocide that day.

CHAPTER FIFTEEN

THE GLUTTONOUS TURNIP OF A MAN

Emma: I got back to the hotel at the same time as Victor was strolling in. He was in flip-flops and long pants, almost as if he'd been out for a morning stroll. I had to remind myself that the last time I'd seen him, he had been dragged away from a fight. It was only as I got closer that I noticed his shirt was ripped, there was a scratch across his face and he had a black eye. The oddest thing was that his shirt was still buttoned all the way up, even though it was flapping open.

He clocked me a little after I spotted him.

Victor Dorsey (son of Daniel and Liz Dorsey, husband of Claire Dorsey): I'm a nice guy. I asked her how she was doing. When she said she was fine, I asked about her dad.

Emma: I said there was no change with Dad's condition, then asked what had happened to him. Vic didn't know that I'd seen everything from the balcony and he said that he'd had 'a disagreement'.

Victor: There was a disagreement. The other guy thought I was a massive arsehole, which was admittedly because I was trying to kick him up *his* massive arsehole.

Emma: He asked if I'd seen Claire, but I hadn't since reception that morning. We ended up walking together through the lobby, out towards the pool. I didn't have much choice because that was the only way back to the cottages. I think he was still a little drunk. He kept giggling to himself.

Claire: I was hoping for a peaceful day by the pool. I had a book about a missing wife to read and, to be honest, being a wife who went missing felt incredibly appealing that morning.

His parents were hanging around, doing their own thing, then I saw Vic walking towards me and I knew it was going to go off.

Emma: It was like one of those Westerns where the two gunslingers walk towards each other. You get a moment where they eye up one another – and then the shooting begins.

Claire: Vic marched over and started pointing in my face, asking why I'd not come to the station to bail him out. I told him the toilet was backed up in our room, so I'd already dealt with enough massive shits for one day.

Emma: I laughed.

Claire: He went through the old hits. I'm a leech. I'm after his money. I'm a whore. He never loved me.

His mum and dad are sitting on one side, with Emma standing on the other. He didn't care. I told him I was flying home.

Emma: Claire points at Vic and goes: 'I am so sick of you.' Then she turned and pointed to Daniel and Liz and adds: 'And I'm so sick of your family.'

Daniel started to speak, but she talked over him. She said: 'You are a gluttonous turnip of a man and the biggest mistake I ever made was marrying into your money-obsessed, piss-stained crotch of a family.'

She then twisted back to Vic and goes: 'You are the worst human being I've ever known.'

After that, she turned and walked off.

Claire: It's fair to say that had been building.

Emma: I thought she had a well-argued point.

Victor: I told her we were finished and that she should pack her bags and go.

Emma: Vic didn't get a word in. He had no idea how to reply.

Daniel: Good riddance to bad rubbish.

Emma: There was a moment of silence where I don't think anyone could believe what had just happened. I thought Claire was off to pack her bags, but when I looked up, she was storming back. She stopped in front of us and then tipped her bag upside down and dumped everything on the sun lounger.

She goes: 'You left the safe unlocked. I thought you might need this the next time you get caught in a gay brothel.'

There was about three or four hundred euros in that pile, plus a gold chain and a couple of other things.

Victor: I've never visited a gay brothel…

…

I've never visited any brothel.

Emma: Vic looked to his dad and then back to Claire and then down to the pile. I followed his eyes – which is when it felt as if the table was rushing towards me. The sun was glinting from the stone and the gold was bright and shiny. I was in no doubt: Dad's emerald ring was sitting neatly on top of Vic's things.

CHAPTER SIXTEEN

THE MAD WITCH

Victor: I know how it looked, OK? I'll tell you now what I told Emma then: I didn't steal her dad's ring.

Emma: I picked up Dad's ring from the pile and held it up to the light. It's so heavy for what it is and there were little bits of dried skin stuck to the inside. I scratched them away with my nail to reveal the 'GM' initials.

Claire: I don't know exactly what happened with the safe in our room – but I can guess. Vic would have tried to seal it but not closed the door all the way. Instead of locking it closed, he locked it open. When I got back from the bar the night we argued, the door was wide. I'd rolled my eyes and thought it was typical of him.

When I went down to breakfast the next day, I scooped everything into my bag, to be on the safe side. I'd not noticed the ring. I thought it was cash and Vic's chain. As soon as Emma picked up that ring, I knew it was her dad's.

Emma: I asked why Vic had Dad's ring. His mouth was hanging open and, for once, Daniel's big mouth was shut. He looked at his son and he looked at the ring and nobody had an answer. Eventually, Vic managed to croak something out.

Victor: I found that ring close to the pool on the first night. I put it in my pocket and didn't think much about it. At some point, I emptied everything into the safe.

Emma: He told this story about finding it by the pool and then nodded across to Claire and went: 'You were there.' Claire was having none of it.

Claire: I had no idea what he was on about.

Emma: Vic's a forty-year-old infant. He's got through an entire life with his parents bailing him out of any problems that might come his way. When he was standing there, faced with facts that couldn't be explained – and even his Dad was silent – he didn't know what to say. That's why he ended up doing the only thing he knows how to do well.

He threw a tantrum.

Victor: I *don't* throw tantrums.

Claire: He chucked a right tantrum.

Emma: He started shouting, pointing and stamping his feet. Some of it was aimed at Claire but most of it came my way. He didn't know who he was angry at. He goes: 'What are you trying to say? Are you saying I pushed your dad?'

Claire: Emma shot right back with: 'You're the only one who said that.'

Emma: Obviously, the gluttonous turnip had to chip in at that moment. God forbid a conversation happens in his vicinity that doesn't need his input.

Claire: Daniel piped up and said something like, 'I'm sure Emma's not accusing you of anything.' That went down about as well as a stripper at a funeral.

Daniel: I was trying to calm the situation. It was obviously a misunderstanding – but guess who had to try to blow it out of all proportion? When it comes to Emma, you only need to know one thing: everything has to be about her.

Emma: If you're in trouble with the law, you have a solicitor speak for you because they're the expert and they know what they're talking about. If I had some sort of issue with gelatinous crustaceans, rampant heart disease, or I wanted to be a massive racist, then I'd invite Daniel Dorsey to speak on my behalf.

Other than that, I'm perfectly capable of stringing together a sentence by myself.

Claire: Emma glared at Daniel, ignored him and then turned back to Vic.

Emma: I asked him where he got the ring.

Victor: I'd already told her that I found it. How many times did she want me to say it?

Emma: Vic's not the sort of person who hears 'no' a lot. If he gives an answer, that's the end of it. Asking him a question for a second time tipped him over the edge.

Claire: I saw what he was going to do about half a second before he did it. He picked up a coffee cup from next to the lounger and threw it across the patio, where it smashed into a wall.

Victor: It slipped.

Claire: He goes: 'Made up your mind already, have you, you mad witch?'

Victor: I said: 'I can't believe you're accusing me of this. I respect your father and would never steal from him.'

Emma: He called me a witch. Claire shook her head and said that's why she was leaving. She actually did walk away that time. Victor shouted something after her, but she carried on walking. Then he threw up his hands and said he was going to the bar.

Claire: I never should have gone on that holiday – but I suppose it cemented what I already knew about marrying into that family. When you're in love – or think you are – you can only see the person in front of you. What you should really do is look at that person's parents. That's what you're going to get in the end. That's what I got.

Emma: I left the gluttonous turnip and his wife on their loungers and finally made my way back to the cottage. It was difficult to reconcile Daniel snooping behind the cottage – and then his son having Dad's ring. I didn't believe either of their explanations but there didn't seem much point in pushing it with them.

It had been such a busy morning – and I hadn't slept well because of the storm – so I had a bit of a nap when I got in. I'd not really planned it, but I'd settled on the bed and then it was suddenly hours later. I only woke up because Mum was struggling to get her key to work in the cottage next door. The metal was scratching the lock in my dreams and then I realised it wasn't a dream at all.

I don't know if it was symptoms of her condition, or that she'd barely slept since we got to the island. Either way, I went outside and she was struggling to get the key to fit. I opened her door for her, then asked about Dad. She shrugged and said they were going to try to bring him out of the coma the following day. I thought that was good news, but she yawned it away.

I remember looking at her and thinking about how I'd never seen anyone look more tired. Her eyelids were drooped and it was as if her entire body was sagging. I had to stop myself from saying all the usual things about looking after herself because it wasn't going to do any good. You can't force someone to eat or sleep.

I think...

...

Maybe I'm wrong, but I think there was a big part of her that had given up. It had been one thing after another, year after year. I know I started it, but it wasn't only me. Her diagnosis and Dad's fall were the final straws.

That's why I almost didn't tell her about Victor having Dad's ring.

Almost.

I handed it back to her and said that Claire found it in their room safe. I also told her Victor's story about finding it on that first night.

I don't know what I expected, but I got... nothing. At most, she blinked. Then she said: 'Maybe your dad took it off?' That would have been fine, except the day before, at the hospital, she'd said: 'He never takes it off.'

I thought about pushing it, wanting her to be as curious as me – but there was no point. In the end, I helped her into the cottage. She insisted I keep the second key so that I could let myself in and out – and then I left her to catch up on some sleep.

Julius: I'd not seen Emma since the previous night – but when I spotted her walking around the side of the pool, I knew there was something different about her. A determination, I suppose. She looked annoyed.

Emma: Julius was on a lounger close to the small pool, where the twins were playing on the waterslides. He was reading a British newspaper in a not reading it kind of way. There were three blonde women in tiny bikinis sunbathing on the other side of that pool and he wasn't being too subtle about watching them.

Julius: Amy and Chloe wanted to play on the slides, so we went to the small pool. I didn't choose that spot.

When Emma came over, she sat on the edge of the sunbed and said that Dad was being brought out of his coma the following day. I'd spoken to Mum as she went past, so already knew that. I figured that would probably be it. We're not the type of brother and sister who say we're best friends and have deep conversations. I've always found those families weird. Emma sighed and didn't seem ready to move, so I asked her if the girls had really been good the night before.

Emma: I told him we'd chatted a lot and he said something about all women loving to gossip. I probably rolled my eyes. Julius is full of comments like that. He's a '*while you're down there, love*'-type.

He wanted to know if the twins had asked me about prison, so I told him that of course they had. They're kids – and kids are always intrigued by the things adults decide should be kept from them.

Julius: My biggest worry about leaving the girls with Emma was that I didn't want them having nightmares about prison. Simone would be fuming if that happened and I didn't want to deal with it.

Emma: After that, he goes: 'Did they say anything else?' I replied: 'Like what?', not knowing what he meant. He didn't reply.

Julius: I thought Emma would go after we talked about the girls, but it looked like she was set. She wanted to talk.

Emma: Mum didn't want to listen, so who else was there? I told him about Victor having Dad's ring and his explanation about finding it on the first night. I was trying to get someone to understand that it was important – but Julius brushed it off the same way Mum had.

Julius: I didn't think it was that big a deal. Dad dropped something and Victor found it. That's perfectly believable. Even if Dad rarely took it off, it was a hot day and a hot night. I have a ring that gets too tight when it's warm.

Emma: I told him about seeing Jin on the cliffs the day before and how he seemed to think that Dad had simply fallen.

Julius: At that time, with the information we had, it was the most likely outcome. Dad had been drinking wine at dinner, gone out to the cliffs for some peace or to watch the sunset, and then accidents happen.

I tried to tell Emma that the reason Jin was thinking that is because that's the natural thing to believe. When Alan fell, the sensible voices were saying the same thing. We were the sensible voices then – now she'd gone the other way.

Emma: I told him I'd spoken to the person in the village who'd found Dad. That he'd heard more than one voice coming from above.

Julius: When you're on the beach below the cliffs, the noise of the whole island swirls around. Emma should know that better than anyone, considering the amount of time she used to spend there with her island boyfriend.

She kept pushing the point, saying someone was with Dad on the cliffs and that Victor had his ring. There was something about Daniel walking by the cottages. There were all these little incidents that weren't connected that she'd somehow turned into a conspiracy. I wasn't going along with any of it, but, at the same time, it felt like she wasn't coping too well with being back on the island. I could hardly tell her it sounded like she was losing her mind.

Emma: I couldn't tell whether Julius was humouring me or if he had some of the same doubts. I don't think we've ever been on the same wavelength as brother and sister.

He was dropping in little nuggets that would feed what I was saying. He said that, when they were at the airport, he'd heard Daniel complaining about Dad's spending. He wasn't clear on details but said that, since Mum's diagnosis, Dad hadn't been as strict with budgets as he used to be. I'd not thought about that, but I suppose the holiday was an example. He'd also bought Mum a new car and I remembered a pair of shoes she'd shown me. There were probably other things.

I figured that if he was spending money to make Mum happier in her final months, then good for him. It was certainly no business of Daniel's.

Julius: We talked for a bit and then the girls wanted to go inside to get some food. They said 'hi' to Emma – and then Emma went back to her cottage. I figured her conspiracy theory would peter itself out. Everyone was concerned about Dad – but I don't know how she thought she was helping.

Emma: I didn't make it back to my cottage. As I passed Mum's, I could see through the window that Daniel was in there. She was supposed to be sleeping, but I'd barely left her half an hour before and he couldn't leave it.

I went inside to find out what was going on and he was talking about some sort of problem with the business back at home. He'd got reception to print out some documents and said something about 'problem tenants'. He needed her signature to cover a bill that had come up.

Daniel: I'm not getting into specifics – but the business account needs two signatures for payments over a certain amount. That would usually be Geoff and myself. With Geoff in hospital, there were two choices – let the bill go unpaid or ask Beth to sign it.

Emma: Mum was sitting on the sofa, struggling to stay awake and he was looming over her, talking and talking. If I'd not got there, I think she'd have actually signed those papers.

Daniel: Sticking her nose in where it wasn't wanted.

Emma: I told Daniel to leave Mum alone and that she needed to rest. Mum said she'd have a look later and that left Daniel nowhere to go. He could hardly continue to pressure her while I was there. He turned between us, but he wasn't going to get his own way this time, so he had to leave.

Julius had just told me how Daniel was annoyed about Dad's spending. If Dad remained unconscious or, worse, if he'd died, it wouldn't be long until Mum had enough of co-signing documents.

She'd have altered the paperwork so that Daniel had sole control of the company.

That's why it was only as Daniel flounced out that I remembered what Scott had said that morning. I'd dismissed it at the time, but there was one person who benefitted the most from Dad falling off that cliff.

It was Daniel.

CHAPTER SEVENTEEN

WHERE IS SHERGAR?

Emma: The phone rang when I was in the cottage half dozing, half keeping an eye out in case Daniel returned. At first I didn't realise what was happening. My phone was charging on the table next to the bed. I picked it up, but there were no notifications. I then realised there was a landline phone on a table close to the door. When I picked it up, there was a woman from the lobby who said that I had a visitor.

I assumed it was going to be Paul – it was only that morning that we talked about meeting – but, when I got there, it was a far less friendly face.

Jin: I don't have a friendly face?

Emma: It was only when I saw Jin that I remembered I'd called him to report that Dad's ring had gone missing. He'd not bothered to call back and so long had passed that the ring was already back. I'd always thought that Scott was exaggerating when he kept talking about botched investigations – but that would be a slow reaction time in a massive city, let alone on a small island.

The first thing I said was that I'd called him and not got a reply.

Jin: There was a lot going on at that time. Other people, other cases.

Emma: He said: 'I'm here now' – but I didn't get the sense he was there because he'd heard my message, I think he'd come to tell me something else. The problem was that I'd already said that I'd called, so he wondered why.

If Dad's ring had still been missing, I would definitely have said – but it felt different now that it was back. If I'd mentioned Victor's name to the police, there would be no going back. I only had that split second to make a decision, but I knew I'd be making an enemy for life if I said what had happened. I could potentially have set our family and Victor's into a full-on war. With Dad and Daniel being business partners, that didn't feel like a good idea. Which is why I didn't bring it up.

I had to say something, though, so I told him I was hoping for an update.

That got a very large roll of the eyes.

Jin basically ignored me and said he needed to speak to Mum but that he thought he'd check with me first to see if she was up to it.

It was… I suppose, in isolation, it was odd. You might ask an adult if a child is up to speaking – but you wouldn't usually do it the other way around. It made me think that he'd been talking to a lot more people than I'd given him credit for. He would have only had to speak with people at the hospital or hotel to know that Mum had been struggling.

I said that Mum needed some sleep, but that she'd likely want to see him if there were any updates. Jin was very tight-lipped at that, so I led him through the lobby and out past the pool towards the cottages at the back. The whole time we were walking, I had a sense that he was already well aware that we were staying there, as opposed to in the hotel itself. I thought about the way I talked to him on the cliffs and realised that I shouldn't have interfered. At best, I'd managed to annoy him; at worst, I'd planted myself directly in his sights for no reason.

When we got to Mum's cottage, I let myself in. I thought she'd be in bed, but she was sitting on the sofa instead, with cucumber slices over her eyes. She called out to ask if it was me – but when I said she had a guest, she grabbed those slices away and looked around, mortified.

Jin: I remembered Mrs McGinley very well. Always so polite… so full of truth.

Emma: It was another meeting of two people who'd not seen one another in nine years. That seemed to be a very common thing that week.

While they were saying hello to one another and asking things like 'How is everything going?', I was busy eyeing the suitcase that was still sitting in the alcove. The envelope that was inside, with the fake driving licence, was now in my cottage – but there was a small voice at the back of my mind saying I should hand it over to Jin. I could wash my hands of it and let Jin deal with whatever it might be.

The only thing that stopped me was that there would be no taking it back.

Before I knew it, Jin was asking Mum how Dad came to end up on the cliff. She said that he liked a walk in the evening, even back at home. That hadn't always been true, but it was something that came about in the past couple of years. I didn't know the precise details, but I think his doctor had told him that he had to cut down on red meat and wine in an attempt to lower his cholesterol. Dad took that to mean he could ignore the doctor as long as he did a bit of walking after dinner each day.

Jin was actually making notes at this point. He went through the list of people who'd come on holiday with us and it was as if his eyebrow got higher with each new name. I could tell that Mum was finding it hard because she kept over-explaining things.

There's one big thing you learn when you're in trouble and need a solicitor – and that's to shut up. If you're asked a question, you should answer it as succinctly as you possibly can, with no elaboration.

When I was arrested, I did not do that.

I don't regret it, because I deserved what I got – but I still remembered the lesson afterwards. I suppose Mum never learned it.

She gave a long and winding reason for why she felt that Daniel and Liz were as close as family, before giving an even more detailed description of Julius's break-up with Simone. By the time she got to Victor and Claire, it was clear to anyone that this holiday wasn't Mum's idea.

She said, 'We're all so close' – and then Jin turned to me to ask if it was true. I had no idea what to say. Claire had just called her father-in-law a gluttonous turnip to his face. His son had thrown a coffee mug at a wall and called me a mad witch. We'd not even been there for forty-eight hours.

I think I came out with something like: 'Some of us are closer than others.' It satisfied Mum – but Jin knew what I really meant.

It was after that when he looked between us and asked: 'Any grudges…? Problems…?' It was very casual, almost throwaway, but Mum answered right away with: 'Of course not.'

The problem was that Jin then turned to me.

Jin: Sometimes people speak the truth when they believe it is best for them. Other times it is because they think it is best for those they love.

Emma: I told him that Victor and Claire had had an argument and that Claire was on her way to the airport to fly home. He seemed largely uninterested in that and immediately came back with: 'What about you and Daniel Dorsey?'

There wasn't a lot I could say, other than that Daniel wasn't my favourite person. Jin poked out his bottom lip and made a note or two. I figured I wasn't telling him anything that he didn't already know. That's the thing about having a loud argument in public: people notice. While I thought Jin had been ignoring my calls, he would have been asking around the hotel. There was one clear thing that anyone in that restaurant knew – Daniel and I did not like one another.

I think that was the reason Mum became unsettled. After I'd answered, Jin turned back to her and asked if Dad and Daniel had any recent disagreements.

Even I was surprised when she started to nod.

Jin: I have the quote here: 'There was a falling-out a couple of months ago. Daniel wanted to expand the business and buy some more properties. Geoff wanted to keep it the same, or go the other way by selling off some assets.'

Emma: It was the first I'd heard of any rift between Dad and Daniel. I also realised how clever Jin had been. He hadn't called me down to reception to ask about Mum's health – he'd done it because he wanted me sitting at his side. He wanted to unsettle me by making it clear he knew about my argument with Daniel. If it looked like there was some sort of rift, Mum would come to my defence by pointing out that it wasn't only me with whom Daniel had a problem. If she had been talking to him on her own, she probably wouldn't have said anything.

It was brilliant, really.

Jin: You British say I'm a botcher. You have the best police. The best laws. The best everything. Well then, let me ask you this: Where is Shergar? Where is Madeleine? Who killed Dando?

Emma: That was the entire reason for Jin to visit the hotel that day. He wanted to ask about Dad and Daniel – and everything else had been a smokescreen.

After Dad had been named as a suspect in Alan's death, I thought Jin was a fraud. I'd believed those stories about a botched investigation, not because I thought Dad did anything – but because I thought Jin had used Dad as a scapegoat.

I spent nine years thinking that and then, in about thirty seconds, I totally changed my mind.

After Mum revealed the falling-out, Jin made a few more notes, closed his book and then said he'd be in contact if there was any more news. He flashed me the greatest eff-you smile I've ever seen – and then he let himself out.

Mum and me sat in silence for a few seconds. I wanted to ask if there were more details about the argument with Dad and Daniel, but it was clear she was having none of it. She'd been holding onto those cucumber slices the entire time and then hurried off to the kitchenette. She dumped them in the bin and then washed her hands for so long that it started to feel uncomfortable watching her.

Eventually the taps went off and she turned back to me. It wasn't tiredness in her face at that point, there was a sort of stoniness… maybe an annoyance because Jin had got the better of her. I'm usually good at reading her – but not then.

She said she was going to get ready for dinner and that she wanted everyone to eat together again. I started to say that Claire had already left, but she snapped 'I know!' over the top of me.

It felt…

…

When that was coupled with finding the fake licence, I think that was the moment where I really started to believe that there was something going on that went far deeper than I was imagining. That going back to Galanikos wasn't simply to give Mum a final holiday, or to celebrate an anniversary or birthday. That there was a reason that went far beyond those things.

Mum told me she'd see me at dinner, which was as close to 'go away' as she ever gets. There was no point in trying to press her any further, so I went back to my cottage.

It was a very strange feeling. You trust your parents, don't you? They're the people who bring you into the world and they're the ones tasked to look after you. It's unsettling when you begin to question those very foundations.

I did what I guess a lot of people do in situations that don't feel quite right: I reached for my phone. The internet is a distraction or a comfort blanket if that's what you want it to be. I wanted the comfort.

I'd left my phone charging when I got the call from reception on the cottage's landline. After that, I had gone straight through to see Jin. So I went to the table next to the bed and reached for my phone… except that it wasn't there.

CHAPTER EIGHTEEN

THE FULL GIANT RADISH

Emma: I know people will be thinking that I put my phone somewhere else, or that it was under the bed – but it wasn't. It was charging on the table at the side of the bed. When I went back for it, the cable was on the floor – but the phone was no longer attached.

I looked both under and in the bed. I checked the drawers – and then walked all around the apartment looking for it.

Someone came into the cottage and stole my phone.

Julius: Emma going on about how her phone had been stolen was the moment I genuinely thought she might be losing whatever plot I once thought she had.

Emma: I used the cottage phone to call front desk and ask them to put me through to Julius's room. I didn't know if he'd still be at the pool – but he picked up. I asked if I'd dropped my phone anywhere around the pool and he said he'd not seen it.

I passed on the message that Mum wanted us to all to eat together that night and asked if he'd tell the others, then I walked across to the lobby myself.

Julius: Emma didn't mention anything about dropping her phone around the pool. She said someone had stolen her phone and asked me to call it. I did that as we were still on the line together. I heard her fussing on the other end before she came back and said she couldn't hear anything vibrating. I assumed she'd left it somewhere.

There's a lot of mysteries from that holiday that I'd like the answer to – but one thing I will one hundred per cent guarantee you is that nobody stole Emma's phone.

Emma: I went to the lobby and waited in line for at least half an hour. A big party had just arrived and people were trying to check in. There were suitcases everywhere and people digging around for passports to show as ID. Someone was arguing about the name on their booking, someone else was saying their luggage had been lost. There was a measured sort of chaos.

By the time I got to the front, I almost felt guilty for having to bother the woman. She was being polite – in the way service workers have to be – but I could tell all she wanted was a bit of a sit-down.

I explained about leaving my phone in the cottage and then it not being there. She typed something into her computer and said she would be right back, before disappearing into the back room.

I think I sensed what was coming. When she returned, she said the only cleaning of the room had happened early in the morning. Those cottages used real keys, not the cards – and the spare key for my cottage was still in place in their office.

It was then I remembered that I'd heard another guest saying that cash had been stolen from her room that morning. I mentioned that – and everything changed. The woman's face hardened and she shot back very quickly to say that the phone had likely been misplaced around the premises. It sounded practised. Like a line that was written down somewhere. She said she'd send someone over to the cottage to help me look.

It was frustrating, sure. You'd be annoyed if you knew something was true but nobody wanted to believe you.

I told her not to bother…

I might have been ruder than that…

…

I started to walk away and I won't pretend I wasn't angry – but then I spotted Scott at the front of the hotel. They keep all the doors open to let the air flow through and I could see out to where they park the cars and the taxis wait.

He was standing there by himself, taking in the surroundings. If he'd been on the cliffs, or next to a fountain – something like that – it would have been understandable. A tourist doing touristy things. But I couldn't understand what he was doing. This is the hotel where we've always stayed – he was here in the past – but Paul told me Scott had a villa. Why was he there?

Scott: I went for a walk that afternoon. It's a beautiful island and the weather was great. Why wouldn't I?

Emma: I think losing something is one of the worst feelings a person can have. It plays with your sense of perspective. Something like a phone can be replaced – but that's not the problem. You try to remember when and where you last had something. It starts to play on you that a fact of which you're certain could be a phantom memory. You gaslight yourself.

Scott didn't see me that afternoon… but it was hard not to wonder if he'd walked through the hotel at some point. Anyone could wander in from the street, especially if they looked like a tourist and had some confidence about them.

Even as I was thinking it, I knew it was nonsensical. How would Scott know I was staying in a cottage? How would he have got in? What could he do with a locked phone?

Why bother?

It was after that when I realised I'd have to go back to the room and use the hotel phone to call the UK and get my SIM card cancelled.

More hassle, more stress – but I didn't get a chance to do anything.

By the time I got back to the cottages, Mum was on her way out. I'd not even realised the length of time I'd spent in reception. I told her I was missing my phone, but she shrugged and said: 'It'll turn up.' She continued walking past me and then stopped and turned to say: 'It's dinner now.'

It felt like being a child again. When your mum tells you to do something with such a tone that it doesn't feel like there's any alternative.

Despite everything that happened on the holiday, those dinners were the one constant. It was Mum's way of keeping away the disorder; something she could control.

Julius: It was a quiet dinner on that third night. Claire had gone, Victor was sulking, Dad was in hospital, Mum was pining for him, Emma was buried in her conspiracies, Daniel had no one to bore with his skiing stories, though he still tried – and Amy and Chloe had tired themselves out by the pool.

Best night of the trip.

Emma: Victor was sulking because Claire had left. He ended up sitting next to his dad and Daniel was busy boring the arse off him by going on about some hunting trip they'd gone on a couple of years before. He was the only one talking at that table and was getting louder the more he drank.

His skin had gone full giant radish at this point. I felt hot just looking at him. He's the sort of man who will walk around saying how he 'always caught the sun', even though what he actually means is that that he's roasted himself for ten hours with no sun cream. The type who'll dismiss all science and government warnings because he's not got skin cancer.

The louder and drunker he got, the more I had to dig my nails into my palms to stop myself from saying something. Daniel was dominating that table with Dad gone. He was finally master of the domain. He'd click his fingers towards waiters to demand more wine and his eyes would follow the women in their short dresses, even though his wife was right there.

When Dad and Alan owned the property business, it was a fifty-fifty thing. After Alan died and things changed, Dad ended up keeping fifty-one per cent, with Daniel buying the other forty-nine. I don't know the specifics of everything – but that's how it stood on that day.

Who benefits? was the only thing I kept thinking. Scott had got that phrase into my head and it wasn't going anywhere.

Julius: Victor left the table first. He said he was off to show a local girl a good time.

Emma: Ugh.

Victor: It was a joke. Everyone at that table knew it was a joke.

Emma: After Victor left, I waited about five minutes and then figured I could make a break for it, too. I had no plans for the evening, other than to call my phone company and then go to sleep. There's that saying about things seeming different in the morning and I really hoped so many things would.

I said goodnight to the twins and Mum – and then walked off towards the cottages. There's an archway a little past the pool, before you get to the walkway for the cottages, where it's almost completely dark. It's only a few steps to get through it and then there's another row of lights. I stood under that arch, looking at the midges buzz close to the lights near the pool, and I felt watched and… vulnerable, I suppose.

I don't think I stood there long, maybe a couple of seconds, and then I walked really quickly back to the cottage. I let myself in and then locked the door behind me. I didn't turn on any lights, but I stood in the window, looking out towards the lawn. I don't know what I expected to see, if anything, but I couldn't lose that feeling of being exposed.

It was probably five minutes until I pulled the curtains and went through to the bedroom.

I saw it the moment I went through, sitting on the side table exactly where I'd left it hours before. Exactly where it *hadn't* been when I'd last looked.

My phone was back.

CHAPTER NINETEEN

THE SECOND GLASS

Emma: Mum woke me up the next morning. I was still dozing when she knocked on the cottage door. She was looking brighter and said she was off to the hospital to see Dad being brought out of the coma. She said she'd contact me if there was any news – but no one was really using their phones on the island because of the poor signal.

There was an optimism about her voice that hadn't been there in a couple of days. She told me to go and enjoy the island and that there was no point in wasting the day.

Perhaps she saw something in my face when she said that. Something I didn't know was there. In the end, I can't tell you why that was the day we finally had the conversation. It had been around three years overdue, but I suppose I didn't want to hear it and she didn't want to say it. Then we were away from our comfort zones and normality and, from nowhere, she finally said it.

She goes: 'It was only two glasses.'

I was standing in the door frame of the cottage and she was about two steps away. She looked right into my eyes, like she was staring into my soul, and her voice croaked as if she was getting over a cold.

I couldn't reply at first, there weren't words. Time shifted. We were suddenly in the cottage's living room area. She was on the sofa, but I was standing, looking down towards her.

She repeated herself: 'It was only two glasses.'

I stared and all I could say was: 'It was still drink-driving, Mum.'

She started with: 'In my day—' but I couldn't listen to that. I talked over her, saying that it *wasn't* her day and that it didn't matter. I shouldn't have had the second glass. I shouldn't have had the first.

If I hadn't been driving that day, then I wouldn't have killed my little boy…

…

…

No, I don't want a minute. I want to say this.

Mum goes: 'It was the other driver who was speeding, not you.'

That's what they kept talking about in court. My solicitor was convinced it was why I'd be dealt with leniently. That's the truth – but it doesn't help. I didn't want leniency.

After the other car hit mine, there was bits of our vehicles scattered across the road. The paramedics was there with the fire brigade and the police. They were trying to cut my little boy free from the wreckage. I should be able to tell you what I was doing, but I don't remember. I never see the scene in moving images. They're always still shots as if I wasn't there. As if I saw the pictures the next day and that those are what stayed with me.

While all that was going on, the other driver and I were both breathalysed. It wasn't in question that he was speeding and had gone through a red light – there was CCTV of it happening – but his reading was zero. Mine was over.

I know that sounds like an excuse, but it honestly isn't – it's a factual thing. I've never tried to minimise what I did. I made a terrible, unconscionable decision to drive.

My baby boy died on the side of the road and then, just after, they arrested me for drink-driving. It all became the same thing.

The papers rightly said I was the drink-driving mum who killed her one-year-old son.

That's me.

That's who I was, who I am, and who I'll always be.

In the three years between the car crash and us ending up in Galanikos, Mum and I had never spoken about what happened and then, suddenly, we were.

I pleaded guilty and it was at the sentencing hearing where the lawyer tried to make the same argument that Mum was later making in the cottage.

Mum looked up to me from the sofa and she said: 'You did your time.'

All I could think was: 'It doesn't bring him back, does it?'

Maybe I said it out loud, or maybe she read those thoughts?

She stood again and went to the door. We weren't having the conversation, after all. She bowed her head a fraction and told me to enjoy the day.

She left after that – and all I can remember thinking is that I really wish we'd not had the talk. It didn't heal anything and it didn't help…

…

I went to prison. I wanted them to throw away the key, but, instead, I was considered low-risk at reoffending, so they let me go after barely half my sentence.

My husband divorced me. Can't blame him for that. I don't even know where he lives now.

They banned me from driving, even though I served that while I was behind bars. Like outlawing a man from walking – but only while he's asleep.

Were there penalties? Not really.

When I was a girl, Mum shouted at me for knocking over a salt shaker. She shouted at me for walking into the kitchen with muddy shoes. She shouted at me for getting home three minutes after curfew. She did all those things and then, when I took away her grandson, she told me that I did my time…

…

…

I need that minute now.

Extract from local newspaper website: '…police said Mrs McGinley had 39 micrograms of alcohol per 100ml of breath when she was breathalysed at the scene. The legal limit is 35 micrograms.'

Emma: I walked down to the village after Mum left and went back to the car hire place. I'd been nervous the day before because I'd not driven since the crash. It was probably that talk with Mum, because I was so furious with her for letting me off, but I wasn't nervous the second time.

I still can't believe I got my driving licence back. If you don't ban someone for life for killing their baby boy, then what do you ban them for?

I wouldn't have reapplied if it wasn't for Tina. She said I might need to drive to help out with the shop at some point, so I did it for her. I never planned to drive again, but then there I was, on Galanikos of all places.

Barak greeted me like an old friend. He told me he'd saved me the best car and that he had the best price. I filled in the paperwork and showed him my driving licence. I was waiting for him to throw it in my face and tell me I shouldn't be allowed anywhere near the road but all he did was photocopy it and hand it back. He barely even looked at it, not that there was anything strange to see. On paper, I'm like any other driver.

Everything took less than five minutes and then he handed me some keys, before pointing to a small white car.

I'd spent so little time thinking this through that it was only when I got to the car that I realised it was an automatic, with the driver's seat on the opposite side to what I'm used to. It should have put me off, but it gave me confidence instead. This was different than any time I had driven before.

It was hot when I got into the driver's seat: that sort of sweltering, suffocating claustrophobia that you only get from cars on a warm day. As soon as I turned the key, cold air started blasting from the vents. I felt the vibrations rumbling and I knew I should be hesitant.

I wasn't.

It was muscle memory as I eased off the lot onto the road. I drove slowly out of the village, but, as soon as you're past the cliffs and the hotel, the complications disappear. The ocean is on one side and the fields are on the other. The only turn-offs are narrow unmarked lanes that lead to isolated houses. Anyone could drive on that stretch of road.

There were no speed limit signs, but I wasn't driving quickly anyway. Aside from bends, the only time I moved the steering wheel was to go around the craters that count for potholes. I'd probably been driving for about half an hour when the road narrowed to a single lane.

When the engine sputtered the first time, I thought it was because of the terrible road surface. Thirty seconds later, it sputtered again. It was like those last few spins of a lawnmower blade after the power has already been turned off. I felt my stomach sink, knowing what was coming.

A few more seconds and the engine cut out completely. The steering suddenly got heavy, not that it mattered too much because the road was straight. The car rolled to a stop, with the front wheels wedged in a pothole the size of a paddling pool.

It was like a cloud had drifted across me, even though the sky was clear. I was filled with this overwhelming sense of dread that comes from being powerless.

I wished there was a real cloud because the sun was searing as I got out of the car. My top stuck to my back immediately and there was sweat on my arms.

On one side of the road, the cliffs dropped down dramatically to the rocks below. On the other, an enormous field of overgrown wild flowers stretched all the way towards the volcano in the distance. It felt as if I was at the edge of the world.

I checked my phone, but there was no signal. I tried to start the car, but it didn't even click. It felt dead. It felt... hopeless.

I looked both ways up and down the empty road, wondering what the hell I was going to do next.

CHAPTER TWENTY

MAYBE A CALIPPO

Emma: I can't believe I'm admitting this – but I opened the bonnet and looked at the engine. I have no qualifications, no training, and I had no clue what I was looking for. I sort of stared at the engine as if that would do any good.

I couldn't see anything, because of course I couldn't – so I walked around the car and had a second look, then I tried turning the key again. Nothing happened, obviously. There was no steam, no fire, nothing obvious… it just didn't work.

The sun was high by this point and it would have been at least thirty degrees. I'd not brought any water. I'd been doing between thirty and forty miles per hour for half an hour, so I was anywhere from fifteen to twenty miles from the village. I was trying to remember the map from the hotel lobby. I'd followed the road up the coast, towards the north, and I had a feeling it was around thirty miles to Agios Georgios. At best, I had ten miles to walk – and that was to a place where there was seemingly nothing. At worst, it was twenty miles the other way to get back to the hotel. Either way, it definitely wasn't a distance that was walkable in that heat.

I sat back in the car, but nothing was working, including the air conditioning, so I left the doors open and then walked across to the cliffs. I kept away from the edge – but I didn't need to be close to see the tide smashing into the rocks below. It was impossible not to think of Dad. How, if the tide had been in, it wouldn't have been a beach where Dad landed. That he wouldn't be in hospital at that moment, that it would have been much worse.

Alan didn't have that luxury. He hit rocks and I guess nobody could survive that.

I was thinking of that when I heard the engine. When I turned, there was a car shooting along the road from the direction of the village. There was a spray of dust and the driver was definitely going a lot faster than I had been.

I dashed back to the road, waving my arms and shouting like a madwoman. It sounds stupid now. It was a single-lane road and there's no way the driver could miss me – the rental car was blocking half the road and he'd have had to swerve onto the verge to go around. That didn't mean the driver would stop – but it *did* mean there was no need to jump around as if I was trying to flag down an airliner.

As the car got closer, the small, chipped stones were spraying off to the side as it bumped up and down across the potholes. I didn't think the driver was going to stop. It certainly didn't seem like they were slowing… and then, as I was about to shield my eyes to escape the dust, the driver slammed on the brakes and bumped to a stop.

I wish I could tell you the guy's name. He didn't tell me and I didn't ask – but he was definitely a local. He was in a vest and trousers, which was one of the easiest ways to know who lived on the island and who didn't. Only people from Galanikos can cope with the heat in anything other than shorts.

He blocked the other half of the road with his car and then got out and looked towards the rental before shrugging at me. He goes: 'Not working?' as if I'd deliberately abandoned the car with the doors open.

I held up my phone and said that the car wouldn't start and that I had no reception.

He was wearing sunglasses and I couldn't see his eyes, but there was this moment where it felt like I could.

I can't explain it, but there was something in the way he looked to me and I felt…

…

I was scared.

Suddenly it didn't feel hot any longer. I was in the middle of nowhere and there was this stranger standing a couple of metres from me.

He asked where I was staying and I must have hesitated because he started listing the hotels in Galanikos. There aren't many and I remember saying 'yes' to the one Paul was in, hoping he would stop.

We stood there for a second and I was in these thin sandals, knowing I couldn't run, even if I wanted to. The cliffs were behind me and, in front, the wild flowers were up to my hip. He was looking at me through those glasses and it felt like anything could happen.

And then he turned to the car and muttered something I didn't understand. He ducked under the bonnet and knocked something with his fist before heading back to his own car. He got a toolbox from the back and then used a spanner to twist something, before whacking another part of the engine with a hammer. He had a bottle of water and poured about half of it into a different part of the engine. When he'd done all that, he stepped away and nodded for me to get back into the car.

All of this happened in about two minutes at the most. I got inside and turned the key – and the engine started. It was like a magic trick. I wanted to ask how he'd done it but knew I'd likely have no clue, even if he explained it.

He closed the bonnet and stepped away, then gave me another shrug as he put his tools back in his car. I was trying to say thanks, but he was already back in his own car. I'd not even closed the door on the rental when he sped off along the road.

I watched his car for a moment, wondering if he might turn and come back. He didn't – he kept driving and, before I knew it, he'd disappeared as magically as he'd arrived.

As well as my relief at the car running again, the other major positive is that the air conditioning had kicked back in. I don't think there's anything quite like a blast of cold air on a scorching day…

…

Maybe a Calippo straight from the freezer on a garage forecourt.

I thought about turning around and heading back to the village. There would be safety there – except that's not where the answers were going to be. So I kept going.

I don't think the road surface got worse – but it certainly didn't get better. Every time the car lurched into a pothole, I thought the engine would cut out again. As patch-up jobs on the side of the road go, that guy must have done quite the piece of work – because the car kept going and going until I came to a small sign that read 'Ag Georgios'.

There was a small row of houses on the inside of the road, with the view unimpeded towards the ocean on the other. The woman at hotel reception had laughed about the idea of coming here – and I soon understood why. There were no side roads and no turn-offs. Within thirty seconds at most, I had driven past the last building and was on the way back out of St George.

I had to stop and do a five-point turn to head back the way I'd come. This time, I left the car on the side of the road and started walking on foot.

I'll call it a village, but St George was so small that I could see from one end to the other. As well as the houses, there were a couple of central buildings that were bigger than the others. I couldn't read the signs on the outside, but there were some tables outside one, so I headed inside.

It was a café in the sense that there was a table with a tea urn and a man sitting behind a newspaper. There was a fan in the corner, but it wasn't doing much other than blowing the hot air around. There was nobody else there and the man blinked up at me as if he was looking at an alien coming down the steps of a flying saucer.

I was holding the envelope that I'd found in Mum and Dad's suitcase, and I took out the sheet of paper that said 'Ag Georgios' across the top. The other scribbles on the page didn't seem to be in English, aside from the '#133'. I felt sorry for the guy when I showed him that sheet. He had this mix of bewilderment and terror on his face. I guess they don't get many tourists out there. Either way, he scanned the page, pouted out his bottom lip and then pointed to the building next door.

It was a strange moment when I walked into that second building. Something utterly foreign and yet something completely recognisable at the same time. The best way I can describe it is when you walk into a neighbour's house and the layout is the same as yours… but different.

That was my first time entering a Galanikos post office.

The first thing I saw inside was a counter with a display of commemorative stamps at the side – plus a stack of differently shaped envelopes. There was a poster with a photo of a passport and lots of foreign writing. It was… strange – and so disconcerting that I almost missed the bank of boxes off to the side.

I only saw them after the man behind the counter said something I didn't understand. There were rows and rows of small metal doors, each around fifteen centimetres square, with numbers on the front.

The man at the counter was still talking, calling at me maybe, but I wasn't listening – because I suddenly realised what the 133 meant – and why there was a key in the envelope.

So I walked across, put the key in the door of PO box 133 – and then I unlocked it.

CHAPTER TWENTY-ONE

THE MAGIC GOAT HAIR

Geoffrey McGinley (husband of Bethan McGinley, father of Emma and Julius McGinley): It'll need more than a drop from a steep cliff to take me out, sunshine.

Emma: Dad's ring was back on his finger when I saw him in the hospital that afternoon. I doubt he even knew it had been missing.

He was awake but drowsy, slurring jokes to himself and trying to get Mum to scratch his backside. Mum said he was on strong painkillers, which was an understatement considering he asked me what rhymed with orange and then giggled himself back to a half sleep that didn't last long.

It's fair to say he wasn't himself... which was apt because I wasn't sure whether I could ever look at him the same way again.

Scott had asked me who benefitted from Alan being pushed – and I didn't want to listen. Then I'd opened the post office box...

I was lost in that when the door to Dad's room opened and the doctor came in. He told us that Dad had multiple fractures in both legs and that operations would be needed to help set them. Before he could finish, Mum asked if that could be done in the UK. I thought it was fairly clear that the doctor was trying to steer us away from that, but as soon as he said 'it's possible', Mum leapt on that and said that they'd get anything done privately as soon as they got back.

The doctor was trying to explain the dangers, but Dad was higher than a hot-air balloon and Mum seemed determined to get him out of there. The doctor said that Dad would need a wheelchair to be on a plane and that they'd do something with his legs to try to make it as comfortable as possible for him.

In the end, he could have said that Dad needed a bed of marshmallows and a pillow made out of magic goat hair and Mum would have said it was fine. She wanted him off the island.

The doctor made a few other checks, gave one final attempt to change Mum's mind – and then wished us well. It was like a parent telling a child not to stick their fingers in an electrical socket and then standing back with their hands up when their stupid kid insisted on doing it anyway.

We sat with Dad for another half an hour or so as he drifted in and out of consciousness. I wanted to ask him about the cliff and whether he was with anyone. If he was, then he never said… not that he said much that was coherent. He pointed at the wall behind me and asked why there were sheep in his room. He asked Mum what was for tea and wondered why there were no spaghetti hoops in the cupboard.

It was surreal.

Mum and I got a taxi back to the hotel, but we were still in the village when I asked the driver to let me out. I told Mum I'd see her later and then crossed a mini plaza and headed across to where the documentary crew were filming. I'd spotted them from the cab and, if you want to know the truth, I was being nosey. I wedged myself behind one of the market stalls and watched as the crew talked to a guy who was running a café. Scott wasn't there – but Paul was. He was holding the boom mic as one of the others asked questions and the café owner answered.

I really wanted to hear what they were saying, especially after seeing the contents of that PO box – but I didn't want to go any closer and let them know I was that bothered. I probably watched for about ten minutes until I looped my way back around the market and headed up the slope towards the hotel.

I wanted to get back to the cottage, but Julius was by the small pool again and called across. I think he might have been waiting for me.

Julius: I'd not seen Emma all day. Amy and Chloe were hoping she'd spend some time with them around the pool. I tried to tell them that Emma wasn't the type of person who'd sit around on a sunbed all day – and I suppose that's how it ended up going. The only times I ever saw her around the hotel were either at dinner – or as she was coming and going.

…

I have no idea what she was doing with her days.

Emma: Julius said that Mum had told him Dad was awake. I replied it was true but that Dad wasn't yet the Dad we remembered because of all the drugs. I suppose, out of context, that could mean a very different thing.

I thought that was it, but Julius nodded me closer and lowered his voice. He said: 'I've been thinking about what you said… that Dad was pushed.'

Julius: I suppose that's what happened – but that doesn't give the context. I *was* thinking about what Emma had been saying, but only because I was worried about her. I wasn't acting like it was a serious theory.

Emma: He asked me why someone would push Dad, so I told him about Daniel and the argument over the business from a few months before. If Dad had died, then Mum wasn't going to bother with the business. Daniel would end up in charge. I reminded Julius that he was the one who'd overheard Daniel talking about Dad's spending.

Julius: She was doing a really good job of seeming crazy.

Emma: I probably talked about seeing Daniel attempt to pressure Mum into signing some papers. I remember Julius and I looking across the pool towards him. Daniel was wearing a pair of shorts that would be obscene in some countries and, if anything, he was somehow redder than the night before. We've had turnip and radish and I'm running out vegetables to compare him against. Maybe a mutant tomato? And, yes, I know a tomato is a fruit. Either way, it was extraordinary. I've never seen a human being that colour before.

There was this moment where Julius and I were looking across the pool at Daniel and I really felt we were on the same page as brother and sister.

Julius: Emma must have seen what she wanted to see, or heard what she wanted to. There was never a time when I indulged her conspiracy theories. At most, I *listened* to her. Does that make me the bad guy? She's my sister.

Emma: Julius said he'd keep half an eye on Daniel, but I wasn't sure what that meant. It sounded like one of those things someone might say. At the same time, it was more than he'd committed to the last time we'd talked. I felt like I finally had an ally.

Julius: Is that the word she used? 'Ally'?

...

If that's what she believed at that time, then she was delusional even earlier than I thought.

CHAPTER TWENTY-TWO

EVEN MORE CHINS

Emma: I was still with Julius and the girls when I watched Daniel stand. He put on a shirt and some flip-flops, then shuffled off towards the cottages.

I followed him away from the pool and reached Mum's cottage a moment after she opened the door to him. Daniel didn't notice me until he'd already spoken – and I suppose it wasn't a surprise when he asked Mum if she'd thought about signing the papers from the day before. She'd been at the hospital all day and he wouldn't have seen her, except for a brief moment when she was re-entering the hotel.

When Mum caught my eye, he turned and realised he'd been overheard. That's when he started saying how fantastic it was that Geoff was awake. He went through the full routine of 'back to fighting fit in no time' and 'he's always been a tough nut', but it seemed so transparent.

Daniel: That girl is like the dregs at the bottom of a wine bottle.

Emma: I think I said 'Mum—' and then Daniel exploded. He spun to me and goes: 'This is none of your concern, girl!'

For me, there are two types of insult. When Claire called him a gluttonous turnip, it's probably something she'd thought up at some point beforehand. I can imagine her sitting on it, stewing, for months or years. Then, when the opportunity arose, she threw it in his face with the fury he deserved.

When Daniel called me a 'girl', there was no sophistication there. Insults like 'boy' or 'girl' are about his level. The only exception is that I once heard him call Victor – his own son, remember – 'as useful as the dregs at the bottom of a wine bottle'. I can imagine him cracking that out roughly twice a week, hoping for a laugh it will never get.

He's not a clever man.

Imagine Piers Morgan with even more chins than he has already – that's the kind of person we're talking about. If it's not 'boy', 'girl' – or the thing that's literally in front of Daniel at the time he's speaking – then he has nothing.

Daniel: You know she's a child murderer, don't you? That's the person you're giving airtime to.

Emma: There was this moment of silence and I think Daniel realised he'd gone too far. It wasn't that he had any concern for me – it's that he'd done it in front of Mum. She didn't have to say anything because she did it all with a look.

Daniel muttered something that might have been 'sorry' and then he told Mum that he needed a decision about money for the repairs. He wanted to scan the sheet and email it back to the UK so that work could begin the next morning. He asked if Dad was up to signing the form, even though I'm about as certain as I can be that he already knew the answer.

Mum said that Dad was on some strong painkillers and wouldn't be up to making big decisions, so Daniel asked if she'd sign it in her role as co-director.

Daniel: This is a straightforward business matter and I have no idea why you're asking about it.

Emma: One thing I do know is that Mum's role in the company is name only. She is a director, but it doesn't come with any role that I know of. I'd guess it's for tax reasons, but it's not for me to say.

Daniel: That is none of her business. Or yours.

Emma: Mum didn't look at the papers before signing them. They could have been for anything. Daniel took them back from her and then winked at me as he turned to head back to the hotel.

He kept staring at me when we were at dinner that night. Every time I glanced up, his piggy eyes would be watching and he'd not bother to turn away. It was starting to feel as if every moment I spent in the hotel was a moment I was stuck with him.

I gave Mum her group dinner, but, after that, I needed to get away.

Daniel: Emma McGinley grew up with wonderful parents and an older brother who went on to be incredibly successful in his field. She can't blame her genes for her failures, which only leaves her personality.

Look at how she dresses, how she speaks. I have no interest in Facebook and all that rubbish – but even I've seen the photos of her on those protest marches. I've seen the disgraceful language she uses while talking about the democratically elected Prime Minister of this country. Did you see what she called people who vote Conservative?

It all came out in the papers after she murdered her son. They printed the lot of it and showed her up for who she is.

If you're asking me to respect a person like that, to *listen* to a person like that, then you're talking to the wrong man.

Paul: When the lobby called my room, saying there was a woman waiting for me, it's fair to say I would've beaten Usain Bolt down the stairs.

Emma: I didn't know whether Paul would want to see me again, but the receptionist had barely put the phone down when he bolted out of the lift. He asked if I wanted to go to the hotel bar, but I was after something more private. The rest of the crew were staying in that hotel and I didn't think it was a good idea for us to be seen together.

We ended up heading into the village. It's easy to get lost there in the evenings. Most tourists stay in their hotels because it's all-inclusive – but even those who don't stick to the bars that are closer to where they're staying.

I knew a few places on the edge of town because Lander would take me there. It's not just that they're quieter, it's that they feel more real. The other bars will be showing football, or other sport that I don't think the locals are too bothered about. There will be pub quizzes, or karaoke… things for tourists.

The bar Paul and I settled into was almost silent. I've never understood those places that have loud music all the time. Literally nobody in the history of humanity has said to their friends: 'Let's go out and listen to recorded music at a volume so loud, I won't be able to hear you speak.'

Paul and I found a snug at the back of a bar. There were a handful of tourists there, but no one either of us recognised. Paul ordered a bottle of the local beer and I did the whole 'Coke, Please,' 'Is Pepsi OK?' 'Yes'-thing.

Paul: Emma was interested in the documentary we were making, which isn't much of a surprise. I told her a couple of things but nothing important. She kept asking whether the end was fixed.

Emma: He pretended he didn't know what I meant, so I had to spell it out. I was asking whether he knew what happened to Alan nine years ago.

Paul: I don't remember what I said in response to that.

Emma: He said a lot without saying anything. They'd spoken to the person who found Alan's body, Jin the police chief, Scott and a couple of other locals that he didn't name. I was fishing for details and wondering if I should tell him about the fake driving licence I'd found with Alan's name and Dad's face.

After looking through the contents of the PO box, I finally had an idea why that licence existed… but I wasn't quite ready to admit it to myself.

Paul: I don't remember things quite like that. She wanted to talk about the film, so we did, though she knew there was lots that I couldn't say.

Then I mentioned that I'd heard rumours someone else had fallen off a cliff in recent days – and that's when she said it was her dad. It was fair to say I was surprised. Speechless, probably.

Emma: I didn't particularly want those worlds to collide – but Paul knew who I was by that point and he'd have found out about Dad sooner or later. It wasn't that I'd gone out of my way to avoid telling him, it was that Paul and I had only seen each other once since Dad fell – and that was on the street with Scott and the rest of the crew.

I told him that Dad was awake, though he had fractures in both legs. He needed surgery and that it was likely he'd end up flying home to have it.

Paul: I didn't want to be the one to say it.

Emma: He didn't mention the similarity to what had happened with Alan, though he must have been thinking it.

Paul: We moved on to chatting about other things. It was either that, or go our separate ways. She told me a bit more about the shop where she works and I told her how I'd got into film-making. It was one of those talks that lasts for hours and yet, at the end, you can't remember what you were talking about.

Emma: I didn't tell him about prison, or the car crash. I thought about it but didn't want to spoil the moment. I thought there was a chance he'd know, anyway. If you search for me on the internet, it's impossible to escape stories of my sentencing.

…

I probably should have told him – but…

…

I think I probably liked him.

Paul: We left the bar and walked back through the village. It was late by then and the sun was all the way down. The market stalls had been packed away and the only sound was the vague noise of music coming from the hotel bars. I saw the village in a different way that night. It wasn't only the front that everyone gets to see, with the all-inclusive buffets and the sun-burned tourists. It felt like a real place, with real people.

We stopped outside my hotel, tucked into the shadows underneath the palm trees where nobody could see us. It was a few degrees cooler. I held her hand.

Emma: He asked if I'd give an interview for the documentary. Ever the romantic.

Paul: It wasn't like that was the only thing we talked about in those shadows. It was a private moment.

Emma: I don't think I want to say any more.

CHAPTER TWENTY-THREE

DAY FIVE

THE DAYS OF PIRATES

Emma: I got up early the next morning. I'd probably only had four or five hours' sleep – but I'd had such a good time with Paul that I was feeling fine anyway.

I walked down to the village while people were still setting up. Café owners were trying to wave me inside, hoping I'd have breakfast, but I waved them away and kept walking.

It probably took around twenty minutes or so until I spotted Lander. He was carrying trays of soft drink cans from the back of a truck into a restaurant. I waited until he'd finished and then asked if I could have a word.

He hesitated and, if I'm honest, I know I probably shouldn't have put him in that position. It was clear that his wife knew who I was and that she didn't want him talking to me. He ummed and erred for a moment and said he'd be about fifteen minutes. When I said I didn't mind waiting, he didn't have much option, unless he outright told me to go away.

Lander: I don't have to do what I'm told. I'm my own man.

Emma: I went to a café over the street, ordered a mountain tea and then waited. Lander came across after about half an hour. He might have been waiting for me to give up and go away – but I needed to talk to him.

Lander: I cannot remember what she wanted that day. Something to do with a bank, I think. We talked, that's all.

Emma: Inside the envelope that I'd got from the PO box was a letter addressed to Alan Lee, with the name 'Bank of Galanikos' across the top. It was dated from more than a decade before, with a series of account numbers listed and linked to him.

I'd been wondering why Dad had an ID with his photo but Alan's details. I couldn't come up with any reason other than that he wanted to move money from those accounts.

It felt as if this was the reason we'd returned to Galanikos, as opposed to anything else. It was all being done under the guise of a family holiday – but then Dad went off that cliff on the first night and everything changed.

That left all sorts of unanswered questions about what might have happened to Alan nine years before – but I had no way of answering those at that time.

I'd also never heard of any sort of local bank, which was where Lander came in. I asked him about the Bank of Galanikos, which, it's fair to say, confused him. He asked what I wanted to know and I said I'd never heard of it.

Lander: I really can't remember what she wanted.

Emma: He asked if I was thinking of opening an account. When I said I wasn't, he went quiet. He said: 'What do you know?' and there was this impasse where it felt like we were speaking a different language.

I'd been visiting the island since I was a girl. My impression of a bank is something like a HSBC, or a Barclays. I thought that

I'd have noticed a branch in all that time. Lander went quiet for a moment and I thought it might be something to do with Rhea and the fact that his wife didn't want us talking. Then, suddenly, things started to make sense.

He said that the Bank of Galanikos isn't something used by locals. There are no high street branches, or special interest-rate deals for new mortgages. They don't advertise on the TV or radio.

He made the bank sound like a myth… something that may or may not exist. He said he didn't know of any branches but that he'd heard it operated out of a fishing village to the north, close to the volcano. It was a word-of-mouth thing that wasn't on any maps. There was no website, no logo or advertising.

Rumours were that people who lived offshore would open accounts to hide money from their local governments. He said it went back to the days of pirates. Boats would turn up with gold and treasure that they wanted stored.

It sounded… far-fetched – especially the pirate bit. But then I thought about stories like the Panama Papers and the Paradise Papers, with rich people doing everything they can to hide their money. And I thought about Dad and the way we had visited this island religiously year after year for such a long time. I'd often wondered why, with all Dad's resources, we kept coming back here of all places.

Then, in that café with Lander, it felt as if I knew.

It felt as if Lander was worried for me after the talk. He reached across and took my hand. His skin always used to be so smooth, but it was rough in that moment. The hands of a man who'd spent nine years doing manual labour.

Maybe I shouldn't have let him touch me – but it didn't mean anything, other than two people who used to know each other sharing a moment. It was comforting.

He asked if I was OK – but it meant more than that. He was asking if I was safe. I wanted to ask what he meant – but didn't get a chance because he suddenly pulled his hand away. His whole body went rigid – and I knew Rhea was behind me a moment before she said his name. She was like a ninja. That's all it took, not even a proper sentence, and then he said that he had to go.

CHAPTER TWENTY-FOUR

THE SOGGY BAGEL

Emma: The crew were setting things up so that the 'Welcome to Galanikos' sign was directly behind where I was standing. It's not a traditional black-on-white sign like the ones from the UK. Someone had painted this beautiful sunshine and beach scene, with the words blended across the top. I had my photo taken in front of it when I would have been eleven or twelve. It was starting to fade, but it was still glorious. I remember I once asked Mum why places in the UK didn't have these types of colourful 'welcome to' signs. I don't think she ever answered.

Paul: I told the crew that Emma and I had run into one another on the street and that I'd asked her if she'd do the interview. That's all they knew about us at that time.

Emma: The cliffs were behind the sign, with the ocean stretching into the distance. I saw the symbolism, obviously. I also knew that Mum and Dad wouldn't be happy with what I was doing. At some point, a documentary would be released, with me as a part of it. Alan was the subject of which nobody dared speak in our family, so I knew a line was being crossed. I wanted to do it, even though I knew the trouble it would cause.

It was Paul who did the prepping. He told me that I could stop at any point and that nobody wanted it to turn into some sort of 'gotcha' interview. I asked if that's what their interviews were usually like and he laughed it away. They all did.

Paul: It was standard stuff. We often take it in turns to prep the interviewees, depending on circumstances. I'd persuaded Emma to speak on camera, so it was left to me.

The interview itself was a bonus we didn't expect. We came to the island to help flesh out what we already had – and then stumbled across Emma and her family. Plus, there was the second story about Emma's father falling. Not to diminish anything that happened – and no disrespect to anyone – but, from a professional point of view, we couldn't have asked for better luck.

Emma: Paul picked up his boom mic and the cameraman did a bunch of light tests. After that, the questions began. There was a lot of background stuff about my earliest memories of the island and how often we came here.

I felt so strange talking about all that in the moment because those memories now felt tainted. Perhaps they weren't cosy family holidays – because Dad had more sinister reasons for coming to the island time after time.

Paul: If she was nervous, then she didn't seem it. I don't remember any particular hesitations and the only breaks were for passing cars and things like that.

Emma: There was a question about whether we stayed in the same hotel every time and I answered 'yes', but then I had to stop myself because there was a jolt of being in a villa that appeared from nowhere. One of those half memories that you can't quite tell whether they're true. I couldn't remember if we'd stayed there or if it had been someone else's and we were visiting.

Julius: I don't remember a villa – but then I didn't go with Mum and Dad every year. I think it was probably just the hotel.

Emma: They asked what drew my family to the island and it stumped me. The obvious answer is sunshine – but you can get that in so many places at that time of year. All I could come up with was: 'I suppose Mum and Dad liked coming here.' I could hardly say that I had a sneaking suspicion that Dad was coming here to launder money. I still hoped I was wrong at that point.

Paul: I thought she was telling the truth. I would never have guessed she was so conflicted.

Emma: That was the set-up and then things moved on to Alan. I genuinely struggled to remember some things because it was so long ago. I remembered more about growing up with Scott. I remembered this epic game of *What's The Time, Mr Wolf?* that we played in Scott's back garden. It must have gone on for hours, in the way those things can when you're younger. We took it turns and somehow didn't get bored. I think we only stopped because it was time for me to go home.

There was an abrupt shift when they asked about Alan falling. I was well into my twenties by then and life was different. I'd been to university and then come back and ended up working for Dad. It wasn't the career I wanted, but it was difficult at that age. Employers advertise for people with degrees – and then want to pay barely above the minimum wage. There was a part of me who wanted to do my own thing – and then another one who'd grown up into this privilege and was seduced by it.

My priorities changed immediately after the car crash. My son had died and, suddenly, those materialistic things meant nothing. I stopped caring about money and, in particular, *Dad's* money.

That wasn't the case when I was in my twenties, though. I wanted expensive shoes and bags. I wanted nights out where money was no object. The only way for me to get any of that was to work for Dad, because he'd pay me a salary that was much beyond anything I could get elsewhere.

…

I didn't say any of that in the original interview by the sign outside Galanikos. I don't think the crew knew about my son at the time. It's not like I lied, more than I stuck to a particular time frame.

What I told them is that I'd probably heard about Alan's fall the morning after it happened. I have a vague memory of being the first person down for breakfast out of our family. That essentially never happened, so I had a feeling something wasn't right. Then Mum came down and told me there had been an accident involving Alan the night before and that it was potentially serious. I'm pretty sure I was eating a soggy bagel at the time.

Paul: The Emma we spoke to by the sign seemed very different from the Emma she was describing. She told us that, after breakfast, she went to lie by the pool for the morning, She wasn't clear about the afternoon, although she said she'd probably have spent some time with a man she knew on the island.

The strangest thing to me in all that is that I couldn't picture an Emma who could lie by a pool for hours at a time. I didn't know her very well – but what I did know about her felt like the opposite of that person. She didn't wait for the world to come to her.

Emma: I was watching Paul when I talked about Lander. I didn't name him, not then, but I was trying to tell Paul with my eyes that I wasn't the sort who came to Galanikos to hook up with people.

Paul: That's not what I thought at all.

Emma: As I was telling them about what I did the day after Alan fell, I realised what a hypocrite I'd become. Liz and Daniel had spent the day at the pool after Dad fell, and I thought they were disrespectful. It took that interview for me to remember that I had done the same.

I think you sometimes need that perspective... not that it changed much about the way I thought of Daniel and Liz. There were so many more reasons to dislike them.

Paul: I'd never heard of Daniel Dorsey at that time, let alone met him. When Emma first started telling me about him, she would do this thing of wrinkling her nose every time she brought him up. It was like she was describing a smell. She made no attempt to hide her contempt for him.

Emma: They asked how Dad took Alan's death – but he wasn't the type of person who'd ever talk about anything like that. Dad came from a generation when they'd ram their feelings deep down inside and refuse to acknowledge they were there. He got it from his dad, I think. It feels like that was the norm back then, but perhaps I'm generalising.

The most I could say is that Dad was quiet for a few days afterwards. There was no big celebration, like we'd often have on our final night. That's about as much as I remember.

Paul: I didn't think it was strange that Emma said she couldn't remember a lot of what happened. Nine years had gone by and a lot had happened to her in those years. When we were doing that interview, I didn't know much of what that was – but, if anything, if I had known, it would have only cemented my opinion. After what happened to her, it's no surprise there are gaps in her memory.

Emma: The complication was that Dad was named as a suspect in Alan's death. The legal system is different on the island and there was a process the police had to go through, which enabled them to interview Dad. I think the closest equivalent in the UK is being cautioned.

Because of that, people instantly thought that meant he was guilty. In the couple of days between the fall and the naming of Dad as a suspect, there had been no issue with Scott. Then, from nowhere, he was convinced Dad had killed his father.

We were due to fly home the day after Dad was named but ended up delaying everything for a couple of days. I don't know the official term, but, essentially, Dad was unnamed as a suspect. The police ended up concluding that Alan fell, but the damage was done by then. A few papers had picked it up back at home and were trying to turn it into a big story of a business rivalry. Once that was out, it was difficult to stop it.

The stupid thing is, Dad was only named as a suspect because he wasn't in his room at the time Alan went over the cliffs. He said he'd gone out for a walk, but there were no witnesses to that. It was all supposition and circumstantial. If it hadn't been for that, things might have been a lot more amicable with Scott.

Paul: I knew what had happened to Emma's father in a legal sense, but it was interesting to hear her side of things. The simple fact is that her father left his room and said he went for a walk, even though there were no witnesses. He really could have been on the cliffs with Alan – but nobody knows except him.

Emma: They wanted to know what happened to the business after that. I don't think they realised that I was working for Dad at the time of Alan's death, so I knew more than they thought.

After Dad was named as a suspect in Alan's death, it was understandable that Alan's wife and Scott wanted nothing to do with the business. Dad needed someone to buy out Alan's half and he was already friends with Daniel, who ended up buying in. Dad bought one per cent of Alan's share – taking him to fifty-one – and Daniel took on the other forty-nine. That's how things had gone for the nine years up until the holiday.

Paul: I remember glancing sideways to the cameraman when Emma said that. We hadn't known any of it. It didn't necessarily change anything – but the fact he went from fifty to fifty-one per cent ownership was something that piqued our interest. It was a motive that we hadn't previously known about.

Emma: When I said it, I think I knew that I'd told them something they didn't know. That didn't mean it counted for anything. They'd have discovered that sooner or later anyway.

Things were winding down after that. Everyone thanked me for giving them my time and then started to pack away. I found a couple of minutes to talk with Paul away from the others and he told me they were all flying home that night.

Paul: I probably should've told her before then, but plans were fluid and… we'd had a couple of good evenings together. I didn't want to spoil things.

Emma: I was disappointed, not annoyed. He said they were going back to the hotel to check out – and then they'd be heading to the airport. He asked if he could take my number so they could come back to me if there was anything to check. I gave him my email address – and then we went our separate ways.

Paul: I didn't think I'd see Emma again.

Then again, I didn't think her holiday would end with an attempted murder… or two, depending on who you believe.

CHAPTER TWENTY-FIVE

THE NO PLAN B

Emma: I was about to let myself into my cottage when I heard Daniel's voice coming from next door. Mum's front door was open and I let myself in. It was turning into this weird form of déjà vu in that Daniel constantly seemed to be hanging around those cottages, even though he had no reason to be there.

Daniel was standing by the alcove, going through the big suitcase on the table. Mum was watching him with her arms crossed, not saying anything as he said: 'There should be an envelope.' He was taking out Dad's clothes and dropping them on the table as he searched underneath.

He spotted me but didn't pay any attention as he kept hunting. It was after he'd emptied everything that he looked back to Mum and asked if she'd moved anything. She said her chargers had been in Dad's case, along with some shoes – but that she hadn't opened it since they'd been moved to the cottage.

That's when she turned to me and asked if I'd seen an envelope when I'd been in the room.

The way Daniel turned to me is something I'll never forget. People talk about the penny dropping and I think that was the first time I ever actually saw it. Imagine teaching a toddler that two plus two is four and then – one day – you see that dawning realisation in their eyes that they finally get it.

That's how Daniel looked at me that day.

I told him I'd not seen an envelope, but it was obvious he didn't believe me and, to be honest, I couldn't care less what he thought.

That's when Mum said that she needed to get ready to go to visit Dad – and she asked Daniel how Dad had seemed that morning.

I think I knew then.

I'd suspected before, but that was the confirmation. Daniel had visited Dad at the hospital – who'd told him to get the envelope from his case.

Daniel: Nonsense. Geoff was ill in hospital. Do you really think we were discussing such trivial things as packing issues? He is one of my oldest friends and I was concerned for his welfare.

Emma: I left after that, partly because Mum wanted us to go, but mainly because I knew it would annoy Daniel.

He was as predictable as you'd expect and followed me outside. Before I could get there, he stood in front of the door to my cottage, stopping me from going inside.

Daniel: That didn't happen.

Emma: He said: 'Did you take something from your parents' room?' I shrugged and replied: 'Like what?'

I was enjoying watching his face turn redder. Then he replied: 'I think you know.'

It took everything I had not to laugh in his face because we both knew we were playing a game. He knew I had that envelope and I knew why he wanted it.

I thought quite carefully about how to reply, more so than usual. I told him that, if I did have something from my parents' room, perhaps I'd be better talking to the police about what I'd found.

Daniel: I told her some home truths that day. Some things that she was long overdue hearing.

Emma: I don't remember exactly what he said.

Daniel: I told her she was a disappointment to her parents and that she should be ashamed of herself. Her father worked hard to give her the best life he could – and look what she did with it. She killed her own son and disgraced her parents' good name in the process. Even when she was released, her dad offered her a way back by returning to the business – but what did she do? She ended up wasting her life in some clothes shop.

Emma: I think he might have said something about the clothes shop, but Daniel doesn't understand anything artistic. He sees value only in money and things that can make him money.

What he doesn't realise is that, when Dad offered me a job back with the business, I was never going to take it. Prison gave me a lot of time to think about my life and who I was going to be.

Now I think about it, I do remember how I replied to him that day. I told Daniel I never wanted to go back to work with him and Dad because, if I did, I'd never be able to sleep again.

I couldn't handle the way they fobbed off tenants. These were people whose homes were leaking and they'd be told it was their fault for drying clothes indoors. They would charge tenants hundreds of pounds for a thirty-quid carpet. They would never return a full deposit because they'd always find something they claimed could be charged against it.

It happened over and over in the time I *did* work for them – and I couldn't go back to it.

Daniel: She doesn't know what she's talking about. She's a child-killer. Her opinion has no worth.

Emma: When it comes to me, Daniel will always take things back to the car crash, but that's the difference between us. I did a terrible thing and I paid for it. He does terrible things every day and carries on as if it was nothing. If he evicts a single mother, it won't even cross his mind that she's a real person who will then struggle for somewhere to live. He only sees that her house is a number on a spreadsheet.

I think he expected me to fold and, when I didn't, he had nowhere to go. He snapped: 'I want that envelope,' as if I would suddenly bend to his will.

I said: 'That's the problem with men like you. People don't tell you "no" often enough.'

He stared at me and I think he was genuinely perplexed by everything. If bullying and intimidation didn't work, then he had no plan B.

Daniel had already taken a step away when I finally came out with it. I said: 'Did you push Dad off the cliff?'

He stopped at that moment and looked back to me. I couldn't read anything in his face and he opened his mouth as if he was about to say something… except he didn't for a second or two. Then he said: 'You're the one with a history for killing people,' because that's the only argument he has.

Daniel: She killed her son. What other argument do you need?

CHAPTER TWENTY-SIX

THE HUMAN SUNDIALS

Emma: I want it to be clear that I never went looking for trouble with Daniel. When I went to dinner, he was there. When I went to the pool, he was there. He was in Mum's cottage and behind the back of mine. I admit that I deliberately wound him up at times – but that only happened because we kept being thrown together. Neither of us were blameless in that regard.

I walked to the village after the argument because there was one thing about Daniel that I'd forgotten I knew. It's strange how things fall out of your head when there's a lot going on.

When I got back to the car rental place, Barak recognised me. He went through his whole 'pretty lady' routine and told me how he'd saved me the best car once again. I could have mentioned how his last one stopped working in the middle of nowhere, but I wasn't after another car.

I asked him how he knew Daniel Dorsey.

When he'd been at the pool handing out cards, there was that moment where Barak had called Daniel 'Mr Dorsey', despite not being introduced. Daniel insisted he'd never been to the island, but it felt like a lie.

I knew for certain it was a lie when I saw Barak's reaction.

He stepped away and picked up a clipboard before making it look as if he was busy. In an instant, he went from trying to offer me a car to trying to pretend I wasn't there. He said: 'Who?' and I went through the spiel of what was said at the pool. Barak started saying that it was a misunderstanding, which was exactly what Daniel said at the time.

I don't think I can explain quite how uncomfortable Barak looked. Whenever you walk past his lot, he would have his arms wide, trying to get people inside. He's loud and personable and remembers people's names. I suppose he could have had other concerns – but he went from that to shuffling his feet and keeping his eyes down.

I kept on at him, saying that he knew Daniel – and that Daniel knew him. Barak mumbled something about not wanting to get into it. There were a couple of tourists on the lot by that point and I could tell he was torn.

In the end, Barak said that 'someone who looked like Mr Dorsey' had been on the island two or three months before. He couched it by saying that it might have been a brother, or cousin – but we both knew the truth.

After that, Barak went off to talk to the other couple and he was back to his old cheery self, talking about the best cars and so on.

Daniel: This is the final time I will say this: I had never visited Galanikos before that trip with Geoff and Beth.

Emma: I know I keep saying that Daniel isn't a clever man – but this is an example of what I mean. It's such a weird thing to lie about. So what if Daniel had been on the island a few months before? He could have said he'd heard Dad talking about it and wanted to see for himself. He could have said he'd read great reviews and wanted a holiday. He could have come up with anything that would have seemed normal. It was the fact he was so insistent on not visiting before that made it suspicious in the first place.

Daniel: People need proof if they're going to make these allegations.

Emma: I went back to the cottage and locked myself inside with the curtains closed. The envelope I'd taken from Dad's suitcase was secure in my safe, alongside the letter I'd found at the PO box. I read everything through and couldn't think of another explanation other than the one I'd come up with.

Dad and Alan had been bringing money to this island over a series of years. After Alan's death, the money had got stuck, and it was only now that Dad was returning to claim it. I assumed Daniel knew about it. I hoped Mum didn't… but perhaps that was wishful thinking.

The thing Julius told me about overhearing money disputes – plus the argument Mum spoke of – suddenly made sense. If there were money issues with the company, then no wonder Dad needed to reclaim the cash that had been left building interest on a foreign island.

There were so many more questions than that. Was it a simple tax thing… or something more?

Julius: Did anyone ever see this so-called fake driving licence?

Daniel: Have you seen this so-called fake driving licence? This list of bank account numbers? Have you even checked that this bank exists? I've never heard of it.

Emma: Another thing I realised then is that nothing was safe in my room. My phone had already gone missing and then reappeared – so somebody had got in and out without me knowing how. By that time, Daniel would have known I had what he was after.

I put the driving licence, PO box key and bank account letter into a hotel dry-cleaning bag and then buried it under a towel in my beach bag. I didn't know where I was going to take it, I just knew I needed to get it away from the hotel.

Julius: Just stop for a moment here. Let's say all this is true: every word of it. Why should Emma care? If there was money that belonged to Dad on an island and he'd gone there to collect it… what's it got to do with her?

Emma: Daniel and Liz always reserved sun loungers in the spot where there's the most sun during the morning. The day before, I'd noticed that they left a second set of towels on the other side and then shifted to those as the sun moved around. It's almost like they were human sundials. You could tell the time of day based upon their position around the pool.

There is no way to leave the hotel from the cottages without going past the pool – so I went the long way around in an attempt to not be noticed. I didn't see Julius or the girls that morning, but then I was walking as quickly as I could.

I don't think anyone spotted me, but, even if they had, I was only carrying a beach bag. I went through the lobby and out the front, before heading down the path towards the village. I was trying to look for somewhere safe to leave that dry-cleaning bag. There's not a bus station as such – but there is a rank where the airport buses stop, and I remembered a row of lockers there. I'd never paid much attention to them but figured I could find out if there was someone in charge and how I could get a key.

I didn't get that far.

I'd only reached the market when I came round a corner to see Scott standing there, haggling with a stallholder over the price for a fake set of Adidas trainers.

Scott: How does she know they were fake?!

Emma: There was this moment that's hard to describe now. I know I've been saying that a lot about various things, but the island does something to you. Everything you might be feeling is dialled up. You don't only get angry, you get *really* angry. You're not simply sad, you're desolate.

The best way I can put it is that Scott looked at me, and I looked at him, and it was as if we were friends again.

Scott: She gave this sort of half-smile and it was like we had never stopped being friends. We were in my back garden playing *What's The Time, Mr Wolf?* and everything in between didn't matter any longer.

I think…

…

I think you had to see her that day to know what I mean.

Emma: I told the stallholder I'd seen the same trainers for thirty euros less on the other side of the market. He looked to me and then back to Scott, before dropping the price. Scott paid up, tipped the guy ten euros anyway, and then we started walking through the village.

Scott: She said she didn't want to argue and that we used to be friends a long time ago.

I told her that I didn't realise she'd stopped working for her dad. I heard that off one of the documentary crew. When I last knew her, she was as much a part of the business as either of our fathers. I suppose I couldn't separate her from her dad.

Emma: It's not true that I was ever as big a part of the business as Dad. I worked *for* him, doing what was largely admin work for an inflated salary.

After Alan died, I kept doing it, but things were changing. Daniel replaced Alan and he was much less bothered about what he thought to be trivial things, such as making sure people had heat or that repairs were done. It was a gradual slide to me leaving, but Daniel and I never got on with one another.

That's why I left the business when I got pregnant. I never intended to go back and I never did.

It wasn't only that…

Scott: I'd found out about what happened to her son by then. After I'd seen her on the street, I'd been really angry and gone back to my villa to do this sort of… hate-Google.

I know that's not a good look.

I searched for her name, hoping to find out that she was some prissy Daddy's girl. Something I could really despise her for… and then I saw all the stuff about her son, and the car, and… the rest. Of everyone I've ever met in my life, Emma would have been last in the list of people I thought might have gone to prison.

Paul: I found out about Emma and her son while we were at the airport, getting ready to fly back to the UK. I was looking for information we might be able to use when we got home – and it was impossible to miss her story.

I know people might think we should have known before – but we'd done no preparation for Emma. We were ready to shoot with Scott on the island. We didn't know what people were going to tell us there, so moving on to her father wasn't in our minds at that time.

After reading those stories, I thought about emailing her – but what would there be to say? She'd chosen not to tell me and that was fair enough.

Emma: When people find out about me, they tend to have two ways of reacting. Some people see the drink-driver headlines and want nothing to do with me. Other people read on and realise it's not as straightforward as it seems.

…

I'm not trying to absolve myself of anything there.

Scott: She'd said I was obsessed with her family. Perhaps that was true for a while, but I didn't know about what had happened to her, which has to say something. If I was constantly checking up on her family, I'd have seen it before.

…

I don't think Emma realises that an enormous majority of people have never heard of her. If you type her name into the internet, then of course those stories appear – but that would be true of anyone. Type your name into the internet and you'll see things that nobody in their day-to-day life would ever stumble across. I bet the people watching this had never heard of Emma until now.

I was living in London at the time she was sent to prison – and knew nothing about her sentencing. The story was more of a local thing. She's not as notorious as I think she believes she is.

Emma: Scott said: 'I read about your son' – and I thought I had misread the situation. I thought he might say something awful… nothing I hadn't heard before but enough to make me stop.

He didn't, though. He said: 'I'm sorry to hear what happened' – and that was it. I don't think I replied. I knew from his tone that I had nothing to fear.

We carried on walking through the market until we were almost at the edge of the village. We were out by the sign where I'd been doing the interview that morning. I don't think he knew about it at that point, but, out of nothing, he said: 'Mum doesn't want me to do the doc.'

Scott: She said going back to the island would bring everything up again. Hard to disagree with that, I suppose. It has, hasn't it?

Emma: He said it felt strange being back on the island, that it was like going back in time. I felt the same. There were so many small things I'd forgotten.

There is this spot in the village where there's a drain cover that's half in the road but half in the pavement. They built around it and it's something you'd never think about – except for when it's right in front of you. When I walked past it, I remembered cycling around that drain cover when I was a girl. Then, from nowhere, you're right back as that little girl.

Scott: Galanikos does odd things to you. If you've never been, then I'm not sure I can describe it. It feels so claustrophobic, as if that village and the hotels are all that matters. Then you leave and life continues. You forget all those feelings until you go back – and then you're suffocated again.

Emma: We sat on the grass a little past the sign. I suppose there's an irony that we were close to the edge of the cliffs, given what happened to each of our fathers. I only thought about that later. At the time, it felt natural and normal.

Scott: When I saw Emma that first time by the car rental place, I thought she'd been coming back to the island year after year. That might have been why I was so angry. I pictured this spoiled girl carrying on as if nothing had happened. All the while, my dad was dead.

Emma: I think the crew had put Scott straight on a few things. He'd been with them just before they left for the airport and someone said this was the first time I'd been back since everything had happened with his dad.

We sat and watched the ocean for a while, or perhaps we just listened to it. I remember feeling this incredible sense of peace. I think I'd forgotten about Dad, Daniel and the rest. It felt as if this was why I was back on the island. Why it was worth it.

Scott: She said: 'Do you *really* think my dad killed yours?' – and it was so earnest that I knew then for absolute certain that she had no idea what happened the night Dad died. I suppose I'd spent years telling myself that I knew, but the truth is that we were in the same position. Neither of us knew what happened.

Emma: He said he didn't know.

Scott: I was angry at the time. I'd gone to bed with a father and woken up without one. Then Geoff was named as a suspect and…

…

Are you telling me you'd act any differently? I wanted someone to blame and the police literally told me: 'Here's the suspect.'

Emma: He said he'd heard about my dad falling and we didn't say anything for a while. When I first saw Scott, I had wondered if he might have been involved as some sort of revenge. I stopped thinking that when we talked on the cliffs. I wanted someone to blame in the same way he did.

Scott: What was there to say? My dad fell off those cliffs – and then so did hers. Is it ironic? It was certainly extraordinary.

Emma: There was perhaps a year-long overlap when we were teenagers where we would talk to each other about things like our feelings. Perhaps it wasn't even that long? Either way, when we drifted, there was a hole in my life that I didn't even realise he filled until that day on the cliffs. It was around twenty years that had passed – but we were talking like the friends we once were. He started telling me about life just before his dad fell.

Scott: I'd always assumed Emma knew what was going on, partly because she was working for her dad at the time. I guess she didn't.

I told her that my dad wanted out of the business. Around three months before he died, Dad started talking to Geoff about potentially being bought out of the company. He was bored of property by that time. There was money to be made – but not the sort of money he wanted. Not only that, he'd already done well for himself. He used to say to me: 'How much money do you realistically need?' I didn't understand it then – but I do now. He was saying he'd made enough. He didn't need to keep buying a bigger house for us. He didn't need more cars, or more expensive holidays. That wasn't him.

Emma: I never knew that Alan wanted out.

Scott: I told Emma that Dad was trying to get out – but that hers wanted to expand. He wanted to buy places abroad and rent them as holiday homes. There was a fundamental difference in what they wanted and seemingly no easy way to fix it.

Then Dad died and the situation resolved itself. Daniel came in and bought Dad's share, while Geoff ended up in a position where he never had to listen to anyone else's opinion again, unless he wanted to.

Emma: I finally saw things from Scott's point of view. No wonder he was suspicious of Dad.

Scott: I know we keep talking about ironies, and maybe I've been misusing the word – but I've got another one here. I'd more or less got over all of this by the time Emma and I talked. I was taking part in the documentary because the team said that, if there was anything to find, then they'd find it. I didn't necessarily expect anything to come up. If they said they thought Dad had fallen by accident, I'd have believed them.

But, as I told Emma about those differences between our fathers, I got this sense that she was the one who was becoming convinced.

Maybe I'm wrong?

Emma: Our conversation was punctuated by these long pauses where neither of us said anything, but neither of us needed to. It was like we knew what the other was thinking.

Scott: I asked her what she was up to now and she told me about the clothes shop where she works with her friend…

…

I'd have never pictured her doing that, not compared to the girl I knew. Obviously, what happened to her son would have changed her… plus prison, of course…

I don't think I have a point here, just that I was surprised. People change, but I suppose you only notice it when you don't see or talk to them in a long while.

Emma: Scott is working as a plumber and owns his own business. I can imagine him being really good at it. He was never the sort to take something on and only do half a job. If he's in for something, then he would try to be the best he could. He said he was taking on an apprentice when he got home because his workload was becoming too much and he needed some help. I was really happy for him.

Scott: I told her I was flying home later that night and suggested we could maybe swap details and get in touch back in the UK. She gave me her email address and told me to message her. I gave her one of the business cards from my wallet, which had all my details. We hugged goodbye and then I headed off towards the villa. I had a bit of packing left to do and then a taxi was picking me up. The last I saw of her, she was sitting on the grass, with a beach bag at her side.

   …

   I didn't see what was in the bag. It wouldn't have crossed my mind to ask.

Emma: It's difficult to know what to make of people who were once so integral to your existence and then, suddenly, they're not.

Scott: How long is it since we were on the island? Five months? Emma has never emailed me since. I sent her one the weekend after I got back. It wasn't anything major, more a: 'Hi, hope you're well'-kind of thing. I probably asked how her dad was doing.

Emma: Scott never emailed me.

Scott: I didn't get a reply and then, about two weeks later, I sent a short follow-up. Something like: 'Hi, did you get my email?' She didn't reply to that either and so I left it. I thought we had reconnected, but I wasn't going to push the issue. She had my card with my phone numbers and email address. All I had was her email address.

Emma: I don't remember a business card.

Scott: You're talking to someone who's been dumped by Emma McGinley twice now. If you're asking if I'd go for the hat-trick, then no.

   …

   …

   Well, maybe. That chat on the cliffs felt like something special. You can't fake that, can you?

CHAPTER TWENTY-SEVEN

THE GENERAL SORT OF AMBIVALENCE

Emma: With talking to Scott, I had almost forgotten that I still had the licence, key and account details in my bag. I was nearly back at the hotel when I remembered why I'd left in the first place.

I then had an idea about a place where nobody except perhaps Lander would ever think of looking. I made a detour to hide the bag – and then went back to the hotel.

I'd barely walked through the doors at the front when it was clear that something was badly wrong. Julius was standing at the reception desk, surrounded by three or four staff members. The manager who'd told me about Dad and moved Mum and me to the cottages was there. He was speaking into a walkie-talkie and there was this manic energy, like when the doors open at a concert and people are excited about what's about to happen.

I'd never seen Julius like he was that afternoon. There are lots of times around family gatherings and the like where I've wondered if he's stoned. It probably comes from the fact that Mum and Dad give him such an easy ride, but he has this general sort of ambivalence to him. As if life is supremely easy.

He was the opposite that day. He was flapping his arms and then putting his hands on his hips, before turning in a circle. He didn't know what to do with himself.

Julius: For the record, I've never been stoned at family gatherings. Another lie.

   …

I've never been stoned full stop.

Emma: I went across to the reception desk, where Julius was and asked him what was going on. He was so distressed that he could barely get the words out.

It was the manager who told me that Amy and Chloe were missing.

CHAPTER TWENTY-EIGHT

THE FOREIGN LOT

Julius: I want this on the record: Amy and Chloe weren't *missing*. That makes it sound much worse than it was. Did Emma tell you that? She's so overdramatic.

Emma: Julius was telling the manager that the twins had been by the pool. He'd gone back to his room for a reason he wasn't clear about – and then, when he returned, they were no longer there.

Julius: I had gone to the toilet. Is that a crime?

Emma: Julius said he'd walked around the pool and then double-checked the room – but that he couldn't see them anywhere. He was definitely worried at this point, although that's no surprise.

He was talking so quickly that it was difficult to understand parts of what he was saying.

The manager called across a few more staff members and then Julius showed them photos of the girls from his phone. The manager sent them off around the hotel to search for the girls.

In the meantime, I dashed over to the cottages. There was no sign of Mum, or the girls, so I raced back to the lobby. By that time, the manager's face was grim. He was talking into the walkie-talkie but turning his back to Julius. It didn't take a genius to figure out what that meant. As soon as I said the girls weren't at the cottages, the manager said he'd call the police…

Julius told him not to.

Julius: It wasn't like that. I knew they'd be nearby and didn't want to bother anyone. Not only that, the hotel staff knew that place better than anyone. They were doing the searching and I trusted them.

Emma: I think Julius was determined to believe that it wasn't happening. If the police came along, it would be real. Without them, he could tell himself they were hiding at the kiddie pool, or something like that.

Not only that, if the police had come, then Julius would have had to tell Mum. You can hardly continue to be the golden child if you've lost your twin daughters, can you? He was more scared of what our parents' thought of him than anything else.

Julius: That's ridiculous.

Emma: I went off to do another check of the pool area. I figured I'd recognise the girls better than any of the staff members who were searching.

It was busy that day, mainly because it was so warm. Nobody wanted to do anything other than lie around the pool. The kids' pool seemed full and nobody was doing much swimming because there was no room to move.

I don't understand how anyone enjoys themselves on days like that. It's so hot and there are so many people. People are always arguing over who has the best sunbeds and how far any of them can be tilted or twisted.

I must have done two laps of the area and didn't see any sign of the girls. Julius hadn't seemed sure what either of them was wearing, which didn't help, but the thought did occur to me that they could be right in front of me and I might struggle to see them. It was hard to walk around because of the sheer number of errant sunbed legs, chairs and the like.

It wouldn't have been my first choice, but I was beginning to get worried at that point – and I stopped next to Liz. She'd again found a way of moving around the pool to keep herself in non-stop sunshine. Given how busy it was, it was quite the skill.

There was no sign of Daniel, but I crouched and asked if she'd seen the twins. I remember Liz lowering her sunglasses so that she could peer over the top towards me. It was proper headmistress stuff – but with the skimpiest of bikinis and a piña colada on the side.

She nodded toward the slides and said they'd been there earlier. In fairness, when I told her the girls were missing, she did immediately jump up and offer to start looking for them. There was this ruthless efficiency about her: shoes on, glasses off, strict march to the lobby. It felt like she might actually get something done.

Liz: Can't trust that foreign lot, can you? You're lucky to get a proper toilet in most of these places.

Emma: I followed Liz through to the lobby, where it was clear the girls still hadn't been found. Julius was following one of the staff members through a door that read 'Staff only' and the manager told me that everyone who works at the hotel was now involved.

Liz was trying to take over, which is when I realised everything I thought about her was true. She kept saying things like 'You people' and 'You lot', which isn't the most helpful thing in that situation.

Liz: Someone needed to take charge.

Emma: While Liz was busy shouting at the manager, I thought of how Julius had told Mum that everything he did was for the girls. I can't explain why it stuck with me, other than it felt wrong. If you see someone trying to do a task left-handed when they're usually right-handed, you can tell something is off… and that's what it was like.

Julius: I don't even remember telling Mum that – but, if I did, then I meant it. Everything I do *is* for the girls.

Emma: I think I'd been caught up in the moment. It was easy to be in that mad sort of panic when you weren't sure what was what. When Liz started shouting, I was able to take a step back.

If I was an eight-year-old girl and I'd been stuck in this hotel for four days, with only brief excursions to the beach – plus I'd been crammed in with all these people on a day this hot – I'd want to get away, too.

And as soon as I started thinking like that, it seemed obvious where they'd be. It's where I'd have been at their age.

Liz: Typical Emma, hey? Couldn't just tell anyone where she thought the girls were. Had to be the centre of attention.

Julius: Emma didn't tell anyone where she was going. That would have been too simple, wouldn't it?

Emma: If I'd told everyone what I thought, and then been wrong, it would have wasted more time. I wasn't trying to be the centre of attention. I don't *want* the attention.

Besides, if I'd not been the one to find them that day, then Julius's little lie wouldn't have been uncovered.

CHAPTER TWENTY-NINE

THE HIPPO TOSS

Emma: The girls were sitting in the long grass, tossing an inflatable ring with a hippo head towards their own shoes. I wasn't sure on the exact rules, but they had assigned each shoe a different amount of points – and were competing to see who could throw the ring over the shoes.

…

In fairness, I've seen worse game shows on prime-time ITV.

Chloe: It was called hippo toss. You get three points for a left foot; one point for a right. Double points if you get two shoes. Triple points if you get both rights, or both lefts.

Emma: I also think they'd stolen the ring from the hotel pool.

Amy: We *borrowed* the ring.

Emma: They were on the cliffs, near where Dad fell – although not too close to the edge. I'm never going to offer parenting advice, but, if it was me, and I was Julius, I'd have taken them to the cliffs before that afternoon. I'd have wanted to see it if I was their age. Kids are naturally curious.

I was about to tell them that they had to go back to the hotel – and that people were worried. I probably should have done, given that I was the adult… but they seemed so happy in the moment. It didn't feel as if I could take that joy away from them.

Amy: Auntie Emma asked if she could play our game. We told her everyone had to pay ten euros to play and that it was winner-takes-all.

Emma: I swear, they must get that smartness from their mother.

Either way, I sat with them in the grass for a while. I watched at first and tried to remember what it was like to live so fearlessly. If there hadn't been a search, I'd bet they could have spent hours in that grass making their own entertainment. You forget all that when you grow up. I can't tell you how much I craved to be able to go back to that. I almost ached for it.

I'd probably been there for a couple of minutes when Amy asked if that was where Granddad fell. I told them it was, but I think they already knew. There was this moment where they both looked across towards the edge in unison. The crickets or grasshoppers were chirping nearby and there was the rush of the water. I could feel the sun prickling my skin and we felt frozen in the moment.

Then Amy turned around and asked if I still thought of Robbie.

Amy: I didn't ask. Daddy told me not to.

Emma: He is… my son… *was* my son…

…

I don't want to say his name any more. Is that OK?

…

It was a question that came so out of nothing that it felt as if she'd run into me. I was winded and the hot, sticky air was clogging my lungs. I have no idea what I told them, but it was probably that my son is always in my thoughts. There is never a time where I don't think about what he might be doing, or how he might be growing.

Every time I looked at Amy and Chloe, I thought of how they were a few years older than him and that he would have been able to follow them around.

When I looked at that kiddie pool in the hotel, all I could think of was how he would have been a little over four years old and that he might have been learning to swim with his dad.

I thought that he'd love the slides, that I'd be mothering him with umbrellas and hats to keep him out of the heat. That he'd have loved the beach balls that people bounced around the main pool. That I could have got him some knock-off T-shirts from the market, and that he'd have liked the man on the corner who stood and blew bubbles all day long.

Every time I saw anything, I thought of how it would have looked through my son's eyes…

…

I probably didn't tell them any of that. I probably just said that I still thought of him.

Amy: Auntie Emma said it was time to go.

Emma: One of the girls asked why people divorced.

Amy: I didn't ask that. Daddy wouldn't have liked it.

Emma: I can't remember whether Julius and Simone were divorced or just separated at that point. When I was young, hardly anyone at school had parents who were divorced. For the generation before me, it would have been basically nobody. I suppose it's different now. I don't know if it's better or worse that people stay together for their kids – but I do know that kids notice and want to ask questions.

I told the girls that sometimes mums and dads don't get on any longer and that, even though they both still love their children, they think it's better to live apart.

What else are you supposed to say?

They knew it, anyway. Chloe gave me a sideways look as if to say: 'Well, duh.'

She then said that Mum and Dad – Julius and Simone – had been arguing a lot and that neither she nor Amy liked it.

Chloe: I didn't say that – and neither did Amy.

Emma: Amy started to say something. I think her exact words were: 'The other night…' but then a look passed between the twins and she went silent. I don't think I've ever seen a single glance that said so much. There was something there and so I told them they can confide in me if they wanted. I wouldn't tell their dad or mum, if that's what they wanted.

Amy looked to Chloe and Chloe looked to Amy – and it was like they were having an entire conversation entirely through telepathy. I've never seen anything like it.

That's when Amy told me that she'd overheard her mum saying that Julius had lost his job months ago.

Amy: I never said anything to her. I want to stop doing this now.

Emma: I didn't get the significance at that moment. I didn't know he was unemployed and I was certain he'd not told Mum or Dad. It might not have been a big deal – except, at the first dinner, Daniel had changed subjects by asking Julius how everything was going at the bank. Julius had said something about a big three months and building up lots of time owing for the holiday. I wish I'd have listened properly, but, at the time, I thought it was Julius being

Julius – and bragging about a load of meaningless nonsense. I didn't realise he was lying through his teeth.

Julius: I've already said this once. I don't think anyone asked about the bank at that first dinner.

Daniel: I didn't say a word to Julius about his bank on that first night.

Claire: I don't remember. I think Daniel might have shouted down something, but I wasn't paying attention.

Emma: I took the girls back to the hotel after that, figuring that I'd promised them they could confide in me. If Julius was lying about his job, then I wasn't going to bring it up with him because I didn't want to break the girls' trust.

Julius was coming out of the manager's office just as we walked into the lobby. He ran across and ended up on his knees, with his arms around both the girls. They seemed somewhat embarrassed, while he was an understandable mix of angry and relieved. He said something like: 'Didn't I tell you to stay put?' before looking up to me and asking where they'd been.

I half thought about lying, mainly to protect them, but I couldn't think of anything better to say than the truth. I said they were on the cliffs, but nowhere close to the edge. They wanted to see where Dad fell – and that I'd have been curious if I was their age. I thought I was helping.

Julius: She basically called me a bad dad in front of everyone. She was saying that I should have dangled them off the cliff, or something like that, because it's the only way they'd have lost their curiosity.

She had some cheek.

Liz: A right nerve on her. Imagine doing what she did to her own son – and then trying to give parenting lessons in front of everyone. Absolute liberty.

Emma: Julius told the girls they were grounded to the room for the rest of the day and then he took them off towards the stairs. They probably got away lightly compared to one of Mum or Dad's punishments when we were young. We'd have had a slipper across the legs, no dinner, and then been made to stay in the room for the rest of the holiday.

Liz was watching me very closely, although she didn't say anything right away. It was as if she was trying to figure out if I'd somehow kidnapped the girls and manufactured everything.

Liz: I genuinely would not put it past her.

Emma: I almost told her to do one – but then she turned around and walked off anyway.

I was about to follow her out towards the pool and cottages when someone called my name. I'd been in such a rush to get into the lobby and find Julius that I'd not noticed the man sitting on the chair right next to the door.

It's fair to say I hadn't expected to talk to him again – but that is when I found out who'd stolen my phone.

CHAPTER THIRTY

THE SMELL OF SOMETHING ROTTEN

Emma: Lander was sitting with his knees crossed, like an old man at a bus stop. It almost made me laugh, except for the way he nodded towards the front door. When he wants to be serious, his eyebrows sink and join in the middle. It was the same that afternoon as it was when I used to spend all my days with him.

I don't think I ever liked that expression. It always meant something bad was about to happen, or that it just had.

I followed Lander out through the main doors and caught up to him close to where the hotel leaves the bins to be collected. There was this smell of something rotten which caught in my throat and I said to Lander: 'Are we doing this here?'

He was in a sort of trance and it was as if he'd not noticed the bins. He turned to look at them and blinked, before we headed off towards the cliffs.

It was the third time I'd been there that day… though I suppose the most open place on the island was also the most private. It's the place where couples got engaged and had artsy photos taken with the ocean and the sunset in the background. It was only minutes before that I'd been sitting with Amy and Chloe – but Lander and I stood. I had no idea what he was going to say, though he'd never been one for talking in circles.

Lander: She told you…?

Emma: He said: 'Rhea stole your phone.' I think I stared at him for a little while, not sure what to say. It was so direct that it took me by surprise. I would've said something like: 'How do you know?' – and then he said that he was the person who'd made her return it to my room.

Lander: I… This isn't what I wanted to talk about.

Emma: I remember the exact words because Lander was pounding his fist into his palm. He said: 'She's not a thief, but she gets very jealous.'

The envy stuff was largely self-evident, although I didn't necessarily blame her. I could see why someone might have a problem with an ex-girlfriend appearing out of nowhere nine years later.

I asked how Rhea got into my room and Lander said she had a cousin on the hotel staff. He asked if we could keep it between us and not take anything further.

Lander: This is a lie.

Emma: Lander said that someone who worked on maintenance across various hotels had been arrested that morning for thefts from rooms. I remembered the woman I'd heard in the lobby at the start of the holiday, saying that she'd had money stolen. I think Paul said something about thefts from his hotel. I guess it was a much bigger problem than anyone had been letting on.

Lander seemed to think everyone knew about the arrest, even though it was the first I'd heard of it. I suppose it's no surprise the hotel was keeping it quiet.

I didn't get his point at first, but after the arrest, the cousin had gone back to Rhea, panicking that she'd be discovered. He was asking me to back away from any complaints about my phone in case it was traced back to Rhea's cousin and, ultimately, Rhea.

Aside from fishing, tourism is the only real industry on the island and if someone gets blacklisted, there's nowhere to go.

Lander: Emma told you this?

Emma: I asked him why my phone. The screen was locked and nobody could get into it. He said it was only to inconvenience me. He saw Rhea with my phone and, when she told him what it was, he insisted it be put back.

...

There was a part of me relieved to hear it. The phone really had been taken and returned. I'd not imagined it.

Lander: I... We... we were on the cliffs to say goodbye. That's all.

Emma: I told him that I hoped everything worked out with him, Rhea and his kids. I said I wanted him to be happy and he said the same to me.

Rhea wouldn't have been happy, but we hugged and it was another of those moments when it felt as if I was slipping through time. It was the way he held me, the position of his hands on my back and the curve of his shoulders. I think a hug is like a fingerprint sometimes. It wasn't that I craved the past, it was that there was a comfort to it.

We separated and then he said goodbye. I think we both knew we'd never see each other again after that. I watched him walk away and there was a closure that I never thought we'd have. If that's the only good thing to come from the holiday, then I suppose it's one thing. Perhaps I should remind myself once in a while that it wasn't all bad.

Lander: I don't know why she'd say all this now. I know nothing about her phone.

CHAPTER THIRTY-ONE

THE IMPORTANT SILENCES

Emma: By the time I got back to the hotel, Mum had returned from the hospital. She was sitting on a lounger a little away from the pool, quite close to the walkthrough for the cottages. The sun had dipped below the trees on the furthest side of the pool and shadows were covering half the patio. The buffet was open again, so people were starting to head back inside.

I didn't know if Mum knew that the girls had been temporarily missing and certainly didn't want to be the one to tell her.

She was on her own, holding a book but staring over the top of it towards the sky. I went and perched next to her, but it took her a moment to notice I was there. When she turned to me, she seemed so… haunted.

I can't think of a better word.

When you're young, you think of your parents as invincible. You think they know everything, which is why you're constantly throwing questions at them. Then there's a strange crossover point where you start to realise that there are issues you understand much more than they do. You notice that they don't know how to adjust something like a toaster, or that the clock on the microwave is always wrong. It's odd little things and you start to wonder if *you're* the grown-up now.

I'll never forget that moment on the lounger, because Mum looked so old and I felt so helpless. I wanted to hold her and be next to her. There's an urge to say everything will be all right, even though we both knew it wouldn't be.

I started wondering if it would be better to lose a parent suddenly, or if this long, winding build-up is the way it's supposed to be. Where you can sit and have conversations about nothing that are really about everything.

We sat for a little while and then she spoke. It was so soft that I barely heard her over the noise from the pool. That quietest voice in the room again.

She said: 'How did you know where the girls would be?'

I was a bit surprised Julius had told her they'd gone missing, but I suppose it would have been hard to keep from her, given the number of staff who'd been searching.

I told her that I hadn't known for certain and that I was only going off what I would have done at that age. Mum nodded but didn't reply at first.

When she did, she had already moved on. She said that the manager had told her she could stay on in the hotel if Dad was stuck on the island. I told her that she had commitments at home, with treatments and doctor visits. That she had to think of herself. She nodded along, but I don't think she took it in. She said that Dad was almost certainly going to return to the UK for his operation anyway.

I wanted to say that it wasn't all about Dad – but I knew she wouldn't want to hear it. She's stubborn and she's loyal… I don't know if those are good things or bad. Perhaps they're both.

Mum and I hadn't talked properly many times since I was released – but that felt like a moment.

I asked if I was a disappointment to her and Dad. I suppose what Daniel said to me outside the cottage had stuck, even though I wanted to believe that it hadn't.

Sometimes, when you say something, you want an instant reply. If you tell someone you love them, you don't want a pause and an 'um…' followed by the inevitable: 'I love you, too.' Sometimes those silences are more important than the words.

Mum didn't say anything for a little while.

She sat and stared out towards the pool before she said: 'Your father understood,' which she quickly corrected to: 'We both understood.'

…

I think I need another minute.

Julius: The thing you have to understand about Emma is that she's always felt like she needs to prove herself to Dad. It's why, when she didn't have that approval, she went so far the other way. She got involved in protests and started taking up causes she knew would annoy him. It's all or nothing with her: if she couldn't make herself the perfect child in the eyes of Dad, then she'd be the rebel instead.

Emma: Mum told me that the crash wasn't my fault and that she and Dad both believed that. The problem was that I don't believe that myself. I knew I shouldn't have got into the car after that second glass of wine – but I did it anyway. If you want the truth, I'd done it before. It's not as if I ever downed a couple of bottles and then drove, but I was never bothered about the odd glass.

Mum probably said two or three times 'we don't blame you', but it wasn't what I wanted. I was still chasing that anger from her because I'd taken away her only grandson. Being blamed isn't the same as being disappointed. I could live with them blaming me for something I did wrong – but I didn't want them to be disappointed with the person I'd become.

Does that make sense?

After a while, Mum said that Dad was far more disappointed that I never returned to the business. She said that, after I came out and was on probation, he wanted me close. He thought it would bring the family together if I went back to the business but, when I said 'no' to that, it was like I was saying 'no' to the family. She told me that he felt rejected…

…

I almost asked her about the fake driving licence at that moment. I wondered if she knew. It felt as if, perhaps for the first time ever, I could ask her whatever I wanted and get an honest reply.

We were both vulnerable…

I didn't.

I asked the wrong question instead. I asked if Dad knew anything about what happened to Alan. There was another pause, but it felt less purposeful than the previous one. More that she couldn't believe I'd come out with it.

She goes: 'Why would you ask that…?' and there was hurt in her voice this time. It was one of those things where the words were already out and it's too late to take them back.

I said a documentary was being filmed about Alan and that I'd met some of the crew on the island. It all came flowing out then. I said that I'd seen Scott and that I'd given an interview. She asked what I'd said and I told her that there was nothing bad. I didn't know anything to say about Alan – and I couldn't remember much from nine years ago anyway.

She was quiet for a long time after that. It was one of those silences that leaves you wondering whether the other person is ever going to reply. You could sit there for hours and hours until someone finally cracks.

I went first. I said: 'Why are we back here?'

Mum replied: 'You know why,' as if it was obvious. The thing is, Dad had billed it as a mix of Mum's final trip here, plus a celebration for their anniversary and her birthday. It was all those things, but it felt like none of them.

I told her that it was Dad who'd brought up all those things, not her. I'd never heard her saying that coming back to the island was a good idea. I had these flashes of Dad standing on a table at the bar, Dad bombing the pool, Dad hiring a golf cart and riding it around the village, Dad betting another man that he could eat five pizzas – and then doing it. In all my memories of being on Galanikos, I wasn't sure I ever remembered Mum particularly enjoying herself.

She took a deep breath and did what she always does when she wants something to disappear: she looked away.

I could have let it go, but I didn't. I asked her how Dad and Daniel had come together as business partners. I asked if Alan and Dad had been arguing before Alan's death. She wasn't answering and I was in the middle of saying something more when she held up a hand. She said: 'I think your father needs our support right now,' before raising her book again.

Julius: Fancy hounding an ill woman like that. Your own, ill, mother. Disgraceful.

Emma: Maybe I went too far? I think that was the time something probably changed for good in our relationship and I suppose I only have myself to blame. Her loyalty was, and always had been, to Dad.

I probably sat with her for another minute or so – but I think I realised there was nowhere to go. This was why we'd never had the conversation in the time since I was released.

I said I'd see her at dinner – and then headed away from the pool towards the cottages. I can't really remember what I was thinking. It had been another of those days where I'd rolled from incident to incident – and I would have been struggling to process everything.

That's why I was already in my cottage when I realised someone else was there.

CHAPTER THIRTY-TWO

THE ASTHMATIC WALRUS

Emma: The front door of the cottage opens immediately into a living room area. There's a sofa and a television, with the kitchenette at the back. There are sliding doors that mean you can leave the kitchen and head directly onto a small grassy area at the back. It's where I'd found Daniel skulking around a day or two before.

The first thing I noticed was that those doors were open. I would close the curtains each morning to try to stop the sun making things too hot – but they had been shoved aside, too.

There was a shuffling from the bedroom – and I already knew what I'd see before I saw it.

Daniel was crouched in front of the dresser, typing combinations into the safe that's built into the largest drawer. He turned briefly to take me in and then spun right back to what he was doing. He didn't care that I was there: he kept typing numbers into the keypad.

Daniel: None of this happened. This is a pack of lies.

Emma: I think I was probably speechless for a moment. It's a bit like when you walk into the cinema and someone's sitting in your reserved seat. You check your ticket and then look at the row number. You might have a look at the row behind and see where the seat numbers match.

I'd almost expected it from him, but it was so brazen and obvious that I was dumbstruck.

I must have said: 'What are you doing?' because I remember him replying: 'What do you *think* I'm doing?' It was like he was drinking a glass of water and I'd asked what he was up to – because the response was so nonchalant.

Each time he'd put in a number, the safe would beep – so there'd be a quick four beeps, a short break and then four more beeps.

He must have tried four or five more combinations as I watched on. It felt like I was out of my body because I wanted to do something, but I felt frozen.

Daniel: Do you know how ridiculous that sounds? She says I was in her room, trying to get into the safe – and all she did was watch! Nonsense of the highest order.

Emma: After those attempts, he stopped and turned to look at me again. He said: 'I need the items you took from your parents' room.'

It wasn't a gentle request; it was a firm order. He's the sort of man who'd like to believe he would be a leader of men on the battlefield when, really, he'd be begging his mum to get him out of having to go in the first place. The bone spurs type.

That sort of posturing doesn't work on me and I told him I didn't know what he was talking about. He glared back and said: 'Yes, you do.' Then he added: 'I want what you took.'

I could have kept playing, but we both knew how things stood, so I told him there was nothing in my safe. He looked between me and the safe, trying to figure out if it was the truth, before he asked where everything was. I didn't answer, so he slammed the dresser drawer and marched across the room towards me.

There was a moment where I thought he might try to shove me into the wall, or do something else. I might have taken a step away. Those cottages are quite isolated from the rest of the hotel. It was only us there.

I'm…

…

Look, I'm not saying I'm some prized fighter, or anything stupid like that. I'm clearly not – but, when you're in prison, you learn a couple of things that can help you. Body position helps a lot more than you might think.

…

I suppose what I'm saying is that I wasn't that bothered about him coming towards me. He's big – but it's not like it's lean muscle.

Daniel: Body-shaming fat jibes. Is that what I'm here for?

Emma: He said: 'Listen, girl, this isn't about you. It's about your family and your father.'

I was ready for that, so I replied: 'I thought I was a disappointment to my parents?'

He bit his lip at that, probably wanting to tell me that I was – but also knowing he wanted something from me.

I decided then that there was no point in holding back any longer and that I might as well try to get some answers. I said: 'Why has Dad got an ID for a dead man with his face on it?'

That was the end of any pretence we'd been going through. He knew that I had the envelope – and that I'd looked through what was in it. He clenched his teeth and moved so close that I could smell the wine he'd been throwing down his throat all day.

He said: 'I want that ID and I want that key.'

I replied: 'I want a lot of things. You can't always get what you want.'

Daniel: I might have asked this before – but did anyone ever *see* this key and ID she's talking about?

Emma: He wanted to know what I'd done with the key, but I suppose he was really asking if I knew what it was for. The only clue was that sheet of paper with 'Ag Georgios' and the PO box number.

I didn't answer, but he must have seen something because he quickly added: 'You've been there, haven't you?'

That was when he really lost the plot. He's not the sort who builds slowly up to a rage. He goes right to eleven. He shouted: 'Where is it?' or maybe: 'Where are they?'

I was in the doorway of the bedroom and told him that he wouldn't find what he wanted in the safe, or the whole of my cottage. I stood aside and told him to keep looking.

He started to seem worried then.

I asked what he and Dad had been arguing about at the airport. Julius had told me there was something about money, but Daniel shook his head and said he didn't know what I was talking about.

He stood in the bedroom, looking between me and the safe, not knowing what to do. I don't think he doubted that I was telling the truth about the envelope being somewhere else. That's when I pointed him towards the back door and told him to get out. I said I'd call security if he didn't leave.

Daniel shuffled past me, huffing and puffing like an asthmatic walrus. He shoved across the curtain and stood in the doorway at the back of the cottage and then said: 'I'll get what I want sooner or later.'

I don't know what he thought might happen, but I said: 'You won't' – and then he marched out.

It would have made more of an impact if he hadn't turned the wrong way after leaving. About two seconds after he left, he ended up walking past the doorway for a second time.

That's the story of him, I suppose. He's a windbag who is all bluster and, when it really comes down to it, he'll make the wrong choice every time.

Daniel: It's the biggest load of rubbish I've ever heard. She should be writing books with an imagination like that.

Here's a question you should be asking. She's created an entire fantasy and conspiracy that's backed by no one but her – but, even within her own rantings, she's admitted she's a thief. If she stole something from her parents, then what was it?

Emma: Doesn't that make it more likely I'm telling the truth? If it was a lie, I could have easily come up with something that didn't involve me taking the licence and key from my parents' room. I told you those things because that's what happened.

Daniel: If this happened like she says, then how did I get into the cottage? I bet she can't answer that.

Emma: I… I don't know how he got in. Maybe I left the sliding doors unlocked, or perhaps the cleaner did.

I don't know.

CHAPTER THIRTY-THREE

THE DYED HAIR AND PERMATAN

Emma: I didn't go to dinner on that fifth night. I didn't want to be a part of Mum's *sit-down-and-pretend-everything-is-fine* party. She knocked on my door, but I told her I was having stomach cramps. I don't think she was convinced, especially after the talk we'd had a bit earlier, but she told me she hoped I would feel better soon – and then she left.

It was the first group meal I missed, though I doubt anyone particularly noticed. Claire had been long gone by that point, plus Dad was at the hospital. The holiday was winding down and I wanted to go home.

Julius: Everyone noticed that Emma wasn't there. Those dinners were Mum's big thing on the trip. It was likely to be her last major holiday, so it wasn't much to ask that everyone could sit together in the evenings. It was maybe an hour out of every day, but Emma couldn't even do that.

It's unforgiveable, really – but then you could say that about so much of how my sister behaved on that holiday.

Emma: I know people will ask why I took the key, the licence and the letter. It's a question I sometimes wonder, though I'm not sure I have a good answer. Maybe it was a sense of loyalty to Scott and his dad? Maybe I wanted to cause trouble? Maybe it's somewhere in between?

Julius: Emma is chaos. This whole thing – the reason she's talked to you and the reason I'm talking now – is an example of it.

If the licence, the key and the letter existed, then why did Emma cause so much trouble by poking her nose into business that wasn't hers? Why didn't she just leave them?

If she's making everything up – which she is, by the way – then she's conned all of you into making a film about her.

You can believe whichever of those two things that you want, but the conclusion is still the same: Emma is chaos.

Emma: I double-checked all the locks and windows before settling down to sleep that night. I also dragged my suitcase into the kitchen and laid it in front of the sliding doors, figuring that someone would trip over it if they were trying to break in.

I didn't sleep much that night. It was half an hour here and twenty minutes there. I tried watching a bit of telly, but all the channels seemed to be full of those adverts that pretend to be actual shows. It doesn't matter where you are in the world, there's always someone with dyed hair and a permatan trying to sell kitchen utensils at three in the morning.

Either way, it didn't feel right sleeping in that room, knowing that Daniel had invaded it. He has a way of poisoning everything he's around. I bet Liz was a relatively normal woman until she ended up with him. I'd barely seen Victor since Claire left him – but you have to wonder what sort of chance he had in life when he had a father like that. Then there's Claire herself. Good for her that she eventually saw through everything.

I was dozing on the sofa when there was a knock on the door. I was groggy and there was a newsreader on the TV screen, when last I'd seen it was the shopping guy with his knife set.

I must have been slow moving because there was a second knock on the door before I could get there. I was bare-footed and in the hotel dressing gown and almost opened the door before I realised I was on autopilot. It was only a few minutes after six in the morning and I wasn't expecting anyone.

When I called to ask who was there, Mum said: 'It's me.' I wondered if we'd ever be able to have another proper conversation – but she sounded chirpier than when we last spoke. I opened the door and the sunshine left me groaning as it surged inside. I was a vampire, cowering from the light, though Mum didn't seem to notice.

She was already dressed for the day with a bag over her shoulder. I had to double-check the time, because she started speaking as if this was something we'd planned. She said she'd had a call from the hospital and that Dad was now off the strongest painkillers. I think her exact words were: 'He's woken up properly now.'

What that really meant was that he was restless and probably annoying the staff. He's never been the sort of man for lie-ins, or going to bed early. He would say he worked hard and played hard – which was, admittedly, an embarrassing thing for a man of his age to be claiming. In his case, there was a truth to it. He hated things out of his control – and I suppose sleep was one of those things. He'd stay up 'til midnight or later and then still be up at six to go to work. It was almost a point of pride for him. Whenever there was some report about people needing eight hours' sleep, he'd scoff and say that he'd been living off a maximum of five for decades.

I think he saw sleep as weakness… like a lot of things, I guess.

Anyway, as I stood in the doorway in the dressing gown, Mum asked if I'd go to the hospital with her. I said I would, and probably would have said 'yes' anyway, but I definitely felt I owed her one after skipping dinner the night before. Those meals were the highlight of the trip for her.

She said she'd wait by the taxi rank at the front of the hotel and then I headed inside to get changed.

Julius: Mum's not the sort of person who would want bad feeling to linger. Because Emma skipped dinner the night before, Mum would have wanted to involve her the next day. That's probably why Mum took Emma to the hospital that morning.

Emma: I don't think we talked in the taxi. If we did, then I don't remember what about. Mum used to talk about Amy and Chloe when there was a break in conversations. She wasn't great with a phone – but the one thing she knew how to do was access her photos. She had thousands on there of the twins that went back years. If we did anything, then it was likely go through those pictures.

The next thing I remember properly is being at the hospital. The morning was stifling and even the short walk from the taxi to the sliding doors left me feeling sticky. The air conditioning was like a loving hug after a long day at work – and I know Mum felt it, too. She caught my eye as we walked through reception and there was a beautiful moment where we were thinking the same thing.

By this point, Mum had spent so much time at the hospital that the staff simply waved her through. I followed her along the corridors until we got close to that door where I'd seen Dad the previous time.

We didn't reach the door.

Dad was bombing along the corridor in a wheelchair, almost giddy with excitement. It was like one of those men you sometimes see in supermarkets, who are hitching rides on the back of trolleys.

It wasn't a particularly high-tech wheelchair and looked heavy and cumbersome. Dad didn't seem to mind as he pushed the wheels as hard as he could and then spun round a corner.

When he saw Mum and me, the grin slipped from his face, like it might do with a child who's been caught doing something they shouldn't.

Perhaps he was still on a certain type of painkiller – but it had been a long time since I'd seen him enjoying something with such abandon. It might have even been one of the last times we were on the island, when he used to bomb the pool. I suppose I'd forgotten that there was still that side to him. He looked mischievous, which is something I'm not sure I'd been able to say about him in a long time.

He wheeled across towards Mum and me, then did this sort of half-skid so that he was side-on. He looked up to me and said: 'Nice to see you, love,' then he turned to Mum and shrugged a non-apology, before saying he'd spent too long in bed.

Both of his legs were in casts – but they weren't the sort of big, white plastered ones I had pictured. It almost looked like two long brown and white bandages that ran most of the way down his legs. I could understand why he'd been going stir-crazy as soon as the drugs wore off.

Dad said he wanted to go back to the hotel to enjoy the last proper day of holiday, but Mum said we should wait to hear what the doctor said first.

It was a long fifteen minutes or so. Dad wheeled himself back to the private room and we followed. We ended up sitting in the chairs by the empty bed as Dad impatiently wheeled himself back and forth across the room. He kept saying: 'Let's just go,' but Mum would give a firm: 'No.' It was all a little surreal. I think Dad was probably still high on the drugs.

I suppose that was why I decided to chance it.

Nobody was talking and so I asked Dad if he remembered what happened when he was on the cliff. It was almost as if I'd jammed the wheels on the chair because he instantly stopped moving. He glanced to Mum and then focused on me. I was sitting and we were at about the same level – although it felt like he was looking down on me. His brow rippled and wrinkles appeared as his eyes narrowed. There was a moment in which I wanted to get away. He seemed so… *focused*, I suppose. Focused on me. I felt like a naughty child about to be told off.

His first words were: 'I wasn't drunk,' even though I don't think anybody had gone out of the way to say he was.

Geoffrey: Before we start properly, I want to make it clear that I'm only talking to you because my son thought it would be a good idea. It sounds like there are lots of wrongs to right and corrections to make. Sloppy work on your part, from what I've heard.

That holiday was supposed to be a time for my wife to enjoy what was going to be her last trip abroad. Obviously, things didn't quite turn out like that – but I will absolutely not countenance anyone saying I was drunk on that first night. I admit I'd had a couple of glasses of wine but nothing more than I might have had on a normal evening at home. I've read the police report, for what it's worth, and it doesn't mention alcohol.

Emma: Dad said that he didn't remember what happened. He was looking out over the cliffs and then heard the wind whistling. Next thing he knew, he was in a hospital bed.

Geoffrey: There's not much to say. I was on the cliff and then I was in that hospital. Accidents happen. No big conspiracy.

Emma: It felt like an anti-climax. The man in the village told me he'd heard voices on the cliffs – but it's true that sound echoes and amplifies around the cove. He could have been wrong.

I felt deflated, like I'd been chasing something that wasn't there.

Geoffrey: I'm still here, aren't I? Cliffs: nil, Geoffrey McGinley: one.

Emma: I wanted to ask more – but then the door opened and the doctor came in. It didn't take long for things to be decided: Dad was going back to the hotel.

CHAPTER THIRTY-FOUR

THE DISHEVELLED NON-GIRLY-GIRL

Emma: I went into the main hotel when we got back and took the lift up to Julius's room. It was early when I knocked on his door, but he was up, watching TV with the girls. I told him that Dad was up and about. It was an obvious slip of the tongue, a stupid thing to say. I blamed it on the early morning and said that what I meant to say was that Dad would be on his way back to the hotel once he'd had the proper paperwork to clear him. It was something to do with needing documents for the airline.

I remember Julius blinking at me, like I'd told him the sky had turned green. He was surprised and I think confused that it was me who'd been at the hospital instead of him. He asked how Dad was.

Julius: It was a surprise to see Emma that morning.

She's never been a girly girl – and I'm not saying that she should be, or anything like that. I'm a feminist, you know. I love women.

But there was something a bit… dishevelled about her that morning. Like she'd slept on the floor, or something like that. I don't think she'd been into the main hotel since that night she babysat the girls, plus she'd skipped dinner the night before. I didn't know if we'd fallen out, or if we were getting on. It's always difficult to tell with her.

Emma: Did he really use the word 'dishevelled'? I don't remember what I was wearing. I suppose Mum rushed me up that morning. Does it matter? Why would it matter?

Julius: You have to understand that was the starting point. My scruffy sister was unexpectedly knocking on my door.

Emma: Julius was acting a bit strangely. It's hard to tell you exactly why, other than that he kept looking past me along the corridor. He said something like the girls would be happy Dad was coming back. It made me realise that I should've spent more time with them since that night I babysat. We'd had those few minutes on the cliff edge, but that was unexpected and I hadn't gone out of my way to plan anything with them.

I regret that. I was wrong.

Julius: I tried to help Emma. I asked her to babysit because I wanted her to rebuild her relationship with Amy and Chloe. Then what happened? She looked after them for one night and essentially ignored them the rest of the holiday. Don't ever let her tell you that the family isolated her: she isolated herself.

Emma: Julius asked if Dad had said anything about what happened on the cliff. It was a fair question, considering it was more or less the first thing I'd asked Dad.

I told him that Dad didn't know what had gone on. I probably could have left it there – but… I didn't.

Julius: I saw it in her eyes: conspiracy time.

Emma: I told him that I'd found Daniel in my cottage the day before. Julius reeled a little at that and asked why.

Julius: Emma said she'd found something of Dad's and that Daniel wanted it.

It sounded, well… mad, I suppose. Such an odd thing to say. I asked what she'd found and she said: 'I'm not sure I should say.'

Emma: I didn't know if I could trust him. It was only the day before that I found out he'd lost his job and had been lying about it.

Julius: She ended up saying: 'It's just something Daniel wants,' as if this was perfectly normal. She'd basically told me she'd stolen something from Dad – and that Daniel wanted it back. What did she expect me to say?

Emma: When it's put like that, I realise it doesn't sound great. All I can say is that it wasn't as clear-cut as that. I knew lots of little bits of information that nobody else seemed to know and I made the best decisions I could in the moment.

It's easy to say I was wrong when you can look back on things – but you could make that observation about all sorts of choices. There's a whole scientific theory about it, called hindsight bias. Say you go into a lake to save a drowning dog. If you drown yourself, it was a terrible idea. If you save the dog and get back to shore, then you're a hero. It's the same decision, but it's viewed through the outcome.

You can say I made the wrong decisions – but what if things had gone differently in those final twenty-four hours?

Julius: …

Really? Dogs in lakes? Is that the best she has…?

Emma: Julius said he was glad we were talking again. I said something like: 'Did we ever stop?'

Julius: She's my sister and there was a double punishment in losing her son and then going to prison. I'm not a monster. I wanted her to be an aunt to Amy and Chloe. Our estrangement, if you want to call it that, was pretty much enforced because she was behind bars.

Emma: I told him that he could have visited me at any time. He said he didn't want to take up any of my visit times when other people could have seen me. He mentioned Mum, but I must have raised an eyebrow or something because he admitted then he didn't want to go to a prison.

Julius: Can you blame me? It's not like we were really close before that. What would we have ever talked about? Surely it was better to let Mum have the visiting slots?

Emma: He said that the twins ask after me and that he'd talk to Simone about seeing if I could be a bigger part of their lives when we got back to the UK.

...

He made me cry.

Julius: ...

Obviously, I know what happened after that – but it was a genuine moment that morning. Amy and Chloe wanted to see more of her and it seemed like they were good for her, too. I thought that Emma might be able to tag along on some weekend trips, that sort of thing.

There were tears in Emma's eyes and I can't pretend that I wasn't uncomfortable. There was a spare toilet roll on a shelf by the door, so I passed it to her and she blew her nose. It led to an awkward moment where she was holding this snotty tissue and didn't know what to do with it. It made us both laugh.

...

I guess that was the last time we really enjoyed one another's company. The last time we were a proper brother and sister. I didn't know it then, of course. If I did, perhaps I'd have thought of something better to talk to her about. If we'd have been flying home that day, everything would have been different.

Emma: I wanted the thing he was offering. I wanted to be a fun aunt. I suppose I wanted to be part of a family.

Julius: It was Emma who chose not to have that.

Emma: We'd been talking for a while and the twins were obviously wondering what was going on. Amy came to the door and squished around her dad. She asked if I was going to be at dinner that night, because she'd missed me the night before. I said that I would. She asked if I'd sit next to her on the plane when we went back, and I replied that I thought she'd want to be by Chloe.

She lowered her voice to a whisper and there was a glint in her eye as she said I could sit in between them.

Julius: Amy came to see what was going on and asked if Emma could sit next to her when we flew home. I said: 'We'll see,' because I thought Mum might want to be with the girls.

Emma: Julius told Amy that we were having a conversation and that she should go back to the telly. He said he'd be back soon and then they could go to the pool. She protested in the way kids do when they want to be involved in the things grown-ups are doing – but she did as she was told, which left Julius and me alone in the doorway again.

Julius: After that, Emma left and I didn't see her again until the cottages.

Emma: Julius moved closer and pulled the door half-closed. He leaned in and whispered, asking if we should tell the police about Daniel.

I think I was surprised more than anything. He had seemed almost dismissive of everything I had been saying – but then he brought up the police.

I said: 'Tell them what?' – and Julius said that Daniel was the person who'd gain the most if Dad had died. That Daniel had been in my room and that something was clearly going on.

Julius: That didn't happen. Emma left after Amy came to the door.

Emma: I said there was no evidence that anything untoward had happened. Bear in mind, I'd never told Julius about the fake licence, or anything else.

He said that we'd be leaving in twenty-four hours and that, if we didn't tell the police about Daniel now, then it would be too late. I said that I wasn't sure Daniel *had* pushed Dad. That even Dad himself wasn't sure what had happened. That it might have been a fall, in the same way Alan had fallen.

Julius: Why would I say any of that to her?

Emma: He stepped away after that and I was so conflicted. There was a while when I thought Dad *had* been pushed and then a time when I was sure he hadn't. Everything had got caught up with the fake licence I found, along with the bank accounts – not to mention seeing Scott and the documentary crew. It felt like a puzzle to be solved and then, on that morning, it turned into a jigsaw that was already complete.

Except that Julius was complicating it. I wondered if I was right in the first place.

…

After Julius stepped away, he said: 'At least Dad's OK…'

That was easy to agree with.

We stood for a moment and then he nudged the door back open and stepped away. He winced again and clutched his side as he was doing that.

I started to ask if he was OK – but it was quickly obvious that he didn't want me to know anything was wrong. I barely got the sentence out before he closed the door in my face.

It was much later that I realised it was that tiny moment that saved me. If it hadn't been for that, I'd be dead.

CHAPTER THIRTY-FIVE

THE AWKWARD, CONTEMPTUOUS TRIANGLE

Emma: I spent about an hour by the pool late in the morning, probably around eleven. Everybody who wants to sunbathe is already up and reserving beds by around seven, so the only spot I could find was near the shallow end, where there was no sun until late in the afternoon.

I read a bit of a book, but, even in the shade, it was so hot that I couldn't think properly. I've always been like that. I like those autumn and spring days where there's a breeze and it never gets above fifteen or sixteen degrees. Sunshine was more Dad's thing, probably Julius's as well.

I said hello to Amy and Chloe – but they were enjoying their final day on the slides, so it wasn't much more than that. They wanted me to join in, but my days of waterslides, rollercoasters and that sort of thing are long behind me.

It was probably around midday when Victor appeared out of nowhere. I was on a sunbed and he stood over me, before nudging the bed with his knee.

I didn't recognise him at first. He was unshaven, plus wearing shades and a hat I'd not seen before. He was also topless, with impressively tanned arms and so much chest hair, it almost looked like he was wearing a vest.

I have no idea what he'd been getting up to in the days since Claire left, but, from the look of him, it likely involved a lot of free booze.

…

Honestly, there was something about him that day that was unquestionably charming. I'd never seen him like that before. He was wearing sunglasses and a fedora that, surprisingly, didn't look ridiculous.

The crackhead rock star look suited him, if you want the truth.

Victor told my chest that something was happening by the cottages and that he'd been sent to find me.

Julius: Everyone was waiting at the cottages except one person.

Emma: When I got there with Victor, Dad was in the middle of a small circle of people. Mum, Julius, the twins, Daniel, Liz and the hotel manager were all there, surrounding Dad in his wheelchair.

It felt like this was some sort of organised thing – but nobody had told me what time Dad was returning, let alone that we were having a mini get-together to celebrate.

Daniel: Typical, wasn't it?

Emma: They were obviously waiting for me. I was feeling out of place and underdressed. Victor had surprised me and I'd forgotten to grab a towel before we headed off to the cottages.

I looked across to Dad and that ring was on his finger, as if it had never left. Meanwhile, Victor was standing a couple of spaces away, as if we were one big, happy family.

When I was in place, Dad lit up, he wheeled himself across to the manager and goes: 'Looks like you have to fall off a cliff to get a good room in this place!'

Everyone laughed, including me. It was a good line.

He wasn't quite the same as I'd seen him that morning, though. I suppose the painkillers had started to wear off.

There was a blanket across his legs and something a little frail about the way he spoke. I wondered what the doctor might have said to him in private, after I left. Whether he'd been told about the timeline before he might be able to walk, or – perhaps – if he'd ever be able to walk again.

I've said before that Dad would never have admitted to any of that. If there was any fear about the state of his health, then he wouldn't have showed it openly – and definitely not in front of a crowd.

I remember him playfully nudging the manager with his elbow and saying he hoped there would be some good wine for dinner that night.

The manager started to reply, but Mum cut him off, saying that Dad wasn't allowed to drink with the medication he was on. Daniel took that moment to open his mouth and come out with something like: 'One never hurt anyone.' It got a laugh, but then he glanced to me and said: 'It's two that's the problem.'

Julius: It probably was out of order.

Daniel: It was an honest mistake and nothing was meant by it. I was greeting an old friend, that's all. This snowflake generation wants to be offended by everything.

Emma: Everyone knew what he meant, probably even the twins. There was a long, long silence and then Dad clapped his hands and said he was grateful for everyone coming out to greet him.

I think the manager probably wanted to get out of there, so he said he had things to do and rushed back towards the main hotel. That was the cue for people to start looking around and head back to whatever they were doing. Victor didn't hang around: he was already past me and on the way back towards the pool when Daniel clamped a hand on Dad's shoulder and said: 'Can I have a word?'

There was something so pronounced about it, so deliberate, that it was obvious he wanted me to see.

I could have left, but I think I knew how things were going to play out. Julius and the girls went back to the pool, while Liz, Mum and me stood in this awkward, contemptuous triangle, with none of us saying anything.

Dad wheeled himself away to the corner of the cottage and, all credit to Daniel, he actually managed to crouch as he spoke to Dad. At most, they spoke for a minute and, as soon as they were done, Dad turned and looked right at me. Daniel was watching me, too.

When he came back towards us, Dad was being deliberately cheery. He thanked me for visiting him in the hospital, and for helping Mum, plus looking after the girls.

It's the compliment sandwich, isn't it? Give all the good information up front, slide the turd into the middle, and then finish with something like: 'By the way, I love that top you're wearing.'

Dad asked Liz and Mum to excuse us and then I was left waiting as they headed back towards the pool.

It was only Dad, Daniel and me on the lawn outside the cottages when he said it.

Daniel: Geoff asked Emma if she was OK. She had been behaving erratically and everyone was worried.

Geoffrey: I'd been at the hospital and hadn't seen everything that had happened. I love my daughter and I wanted her to be well.

Emma: Dad told me that I had to return what I'd taken from his room. He wanted me to give it to Daniel.

I'd guessed before – but that was the moment I knew for sure that Dad and Daniel were in it together. I asked what they were up to.

Geoffrey: I wish I could tell you that the conversation went like that – but my daughter has a wild imagination.

Emma: Dad wouldn't say – and neither would Daniel. I wanted to try to get something, anything, out of them, so I said: 'I think Daniel might have pushed you off the cliff.'

Daniel was right there. I said it to his face.

Geoffrey: Emma said things that she might regret now. I hope she does.

Emma: Dad said 'no'. I asked again what was going on – but he said it was none of my business. I said it *was* my business if he wanted me to return it.

He blew then.

Geoffrey: I had just returned from hospital and the last thing I wanted was to deal with a daughter who was having… *problems*.

Emma: He shouted: 'You *stole* it.'

It was true, I suppose… but it felt like he'd stolen from me, too. That the childhood memories I had of being on the island were no longer true. They weren't family holidays for us to enjoy together – there was something going on under the surface that I'd known nothing about.

I said that I needed to put on some clothes – and there was satisfaction in making them wait as I went into my cottage.

My suitcase was still on the floor by the sliding doors in the kitchen and I grabbed a cardigan, before I stood and waited under the vents for a short while. It was cooler inside and my thoughts felt sharper.

I could have sneaked out the back and made some sort of run for it. Dad was in a wheelchair and Daniel couldn't catch an arthritic sloth. I don't know where I would have gone – but I wouldn't have had to listen to them.

I thought about it.

I didn't, though.

I went back through the cottage until I was on the lawn with Daniel and Dad. I told Dad I could take what I'd found to the police. I think they'd half thought I might have been going into the cottage to fetch the envelope – and the second of silence made it clear my continued disobedience wasn't what they expected.

Dad said: 'You wouldn't,' so I told him I absolutely would, unless he told me what was going on.

Daniel and Dad exchanged a look and it felt like they'd been talking while I was away. They didn't need to say anything more because they had already decided.

Dad nodded to his cottage and said: 'Inside.'

I felt like a little girl then, as if I'd been grounded. I was almost past him when Dad coughed and I realised he wanted me to wheel him inside.

It felt strange doing that. I had never pushed anyone in a wheelchair before and the chair would have been heavy, even without Dad in it. Those few seconds gave me the tiniest glimpse into what it must be like for someone who's disabled. I had to open their front door, find something to wedge it in place, then go back and wheel Dad across the lawn, over the path and through the threshold. It would have taken me five seconds to walk by myself, but probably took at least two minutes to do everything. I was gasping by the end, not as fit as I thought.

A part of me pictured this life for Dad in future – and I knew it would drive him mad. Any novelty there might be because of the wheelchair would wear off the moment he had to try to get upstairs in his house. I wondered if they might shift the main bedroom to somewhere downstairs, or if he'd need someone to drive him around for a while. Or forever.

I felt sorry for him – but I was so angry, too.

Daniel hadn't followed us in, so it was just me and Dad. He bumped himself into the corner of the table by accident and then spent a few seconds trying to turn himself around. By this time, he was getting frustrated with the chair as well as me. I felt power, knowing I could walk away from him because of his condition – but knew it would be awful to do that.

Geoffrey: I've read the transcript of what my daughter told you and don't know what else to say, other than that there is no truth within it.

We did talk in the cottage that afternoon – but not about the things she mentioned. I said that I hoped we could get back on track as a family and that I forgave her.

I've considered legal action over her claims – but have decided that the weight of evidence against her statements should be enough to speak for itself.

I do not want to sue my daughter – and you are lucky in the sense that you are protected through her.

Emma: Dad told me that he and Daniel had money invested on the island, which is something I'd more or less figured out by that point.

I asked him why he had the fake driving licence, which is when he explained that Alan had opened accounts years before. After he died, the business' money was stuck. Only Alan could withdraw, except that Alan was dead. It took him nine years to come up with a plan to get it – and, even then, I figured it was spurred on because of Mum's condition and his resulting spending spree.

None of that was a surprise – but I suppose the barefacedness was. He was literally trying to do the thing I thought he was: rob a bank.

It also answered the question as to why Barak knew Daniel. Daniel would have come to the island a while before to try to claim the money. He'd have needed a car to get to wherever the bank was. Lander mentioned the fishing villages to the north, near the volcano.

Once Daniel got there and realised he needed an ID he couldn't possibly have, he'd gone home and hatched the rest with Dad. Somehow, they had got hold of a fake driving licence – and here we were. They were all set to claim the money, except that Dad went over that cliff and everything was at risk again.

That's when I knew for certain that Daniel had nothing to do with Dad falling. It was the opposite of what he would have wanted. He needed Dad to claim the money for the business.

I couldn't help but think of what Lander had told me – that there were no branches on the street and that the Bank of Galanikos was almost a myth of an institution. It was only useful for people wanting to hide money.

I asked Dad why he needed a bank account on the island and that's when he started scratching his arms. It wasn't a casual brush, he was digging in his nails and raking them, to the point that I could see red marks. I asked if he was all right, but his head twitched, as if he had some sort of tic.

It was… frightening, I suppose. I didn't know what to do and ended up hurrying across to him and trying to hold his hand. I kept saying 'Dad', but his eyes were glazed and his attention gone. I was ready to start shouting, to try to get him help, but then, from nowhere, he was back. His eyes zeroed in on me and he grabbed my wrist so hard that I could see the veins bulging in his forearm.

It hurt.

He was squeezing so tight, that it was like he was trying to rip off my hand. By the time I pulled away, there were fingermarks embedded in my skin.

He said: 'Give it back' – and he wasn't messing. I'm not sure he's ever spoken to me like that before. It was pure anger. His eyes were narrow and his nostrils flared.

I hadn't been frightened of Daniel – but I was scared of Dad in that moment. Any thoughts I had of continuing to do my own thing were gone.

It was one of those moments where you realise afterwards that things can never quite be the same again. I'd never been hit by either of my parents – it wasn't that sort of upbringing – but a line was crossed that day.

Julius: I never saw any marks on Emma's wrist when we were at dinner later that day. If it was as bad as she claims, surely there would have been something…?

Emma: Dad must've realised what he'd done. I was rubbing my wrist and probably a bit emotional. He said 'sorry' – and then there was a stand-off for a few seconds. I don't know if he was worried about me, or worried that I wouldn't give him what he wanted.

He started to tell me that the money on the island was 'investments', but that felt like such a cop-out. I asked why a straightforward 'investment' couldn't have been put in a British bank, which didn't get much of a reply. I asked where the money had come from in the first place – but that didn't get an answer, either. I think the lack of an answer probably said more than an actual one. It clearly wasn't money from their rentals back in the UK.

We were at a stand-off again. I didn't know what to say because it was clear I wasn't going to get a better reply.

Dad said 'give it back' – and that was the end of the conversation. I walked out of the cottage without another word.

What happened next is a bit of a blur. I think I ran out of the hotel – and yet I don't remember changing into proper shoes and I doubt I would have run in sandals.

The dry-cleaning bag with the account numbers, key, and driving licence was hidden in the ruins of the abandoned, unfinished Grand Paradise Hotel. It's like I was outside Dad's cottage and then, the next moment, I was at the Grand Paradise.

The grass was up to my waist and the unfinished walls were crumbling. The heat felt more intense out there and the sound of the crickets was deafening.

There were so many places to hide things on that site – and also no reason for anyone to go there. I'd tucked the bag underneath a pile of bricks, where nobody would have found it unless they knew it was there. When I pulled it out, it was as if it had never been left. The bag was clean and the contents untouched.

I walked back to the hotel and kept going through the lobby until I was at Dad's cottage. I let myself in with the key Mum had given me – and she was in there this time. She was on the sofa, with Dad sitting across from her in the wheelchair. They both looked up to me and it felt like the end of something.

I put the cottage key on the table and then dropped the dry-cleaning bag onto Dad's lap. He didn't check it, he simply said a quiet 'thank you'.

I was looking at Mum the entire time, wondering if she knew, or approved. Wondering if she cared.

I said: 'Is this why we're here? It's nothing to do with Mum's final trip, or an anniversary, or birthday. We're here for money…?'

Mum looked at the floor and Dad didn't answer. We stood there, saying nothing to one another – because what was there to say?

My family was a lie – and it had taken me three decades to work it out.

CHAPTER THIRTY-SIX

THE TWO STRANGLED CATS

Emma: Mum knocked on the door to my cottage a few minutes before half-past seven that night. She was dressed for dinner and she stood there for a moment, before she said: 'Will you come?'

With the exception of the twins, I wasn't sure I wanted to see any of them again. I certainly didn't want to listen to Dad and Daniel backslapping one another and reminiscing about old times.

I couldn't let down Mum, though.

It was our final night on the island and there was a good chance it would be the last time we all sat down together.

I put on my shoes and then Mum and I walked across to the hotel restaurant together. The evening was a bit cooler than the previous ones. The sun had dipped across the other side of the hotel and orange was starting to spread across the sky.

The pool was silent, except for the gentle hum of the filter. The restaurant had its own soundtrack: the scraping of chairs and cutlery, the clinking of glasses and the low rumble of chatter. It felt ominous as I was walking there, but I'm not sure I can tell you why. Maybe it was those memories of a prison canteen, or perhaps I knew something was going to happen that night?

Julius: Everyone was waiting for Emma – and even Victor had got there on time. It was our final night – plus Dad's first one back from hospital. I think everyone except her was up for having a good time.

Emma: Dad was at the head of the table, with Mum on one side and Julius on the other. There was a space next to Mum, so I sat with her on my left, and Victor on the right. The twins were opposite me, with Daniel and Liz further down the table.

All of that became so important in the end. I was certainly happy that I wouldn't have to tolerate Daniel all night.

It felt happy and jovial, I suppose, although I was feeling none of that. I wanted to leave – and would have already gone if it wasn't for the fact that I couldn't afford a new flight home. I was going to have to wait until the next day, like everyone else.

I had just sat when Mum touched my hand and asked if I'd fill up Dad's plate for him. I almost said he could do it himself – but then remembered the wheelchair, plus the fact that I wanted Mum to enjoy her last night.

I squeezed her shoulder gently and then headed across to the buffet. There's a stack of clean plates, so I took two and then got in line.

That time of day is the most popular for eating and there was a long stream of people shuffling along. There's always someone who seemingly can't figure out how tongs work, or who wanders off with the spoon that's meant to be used for scooping pasta. Someone is having a breakdown because there is a temporary shortage of potatoes, or there's a person who will only eat margherita pizza.

I could easily live with never seeing another buffet again. It's another of those things that bring out the worst in people.

I was near the front when Julius slotted in alongside me. He'd skipped the line and made it look as if I'd let him in. He was holding two plates as well, saying that he was getting food for Mum.

I probably asked how the twins were, but perhaps we didn't speak at all? I don't remember much other than shuffling along in the line.

When we got to the front, I loaded Dad's plate with the same pork paella that I got him on the first night. I put on a small scoop of chips, plus some chunks of meat. I don't remember what I got for myself – but I doubt it was much. Julius was next to me the whole time, loading up his pair of plates. I wish I'd paid more attention to what he was doing – but who would? It's the drowning dog again – decisions we make seem so different in retrospect.

Julius and I got back to the table at the same time and we spread around the four plates. Dad saw the rice I'd got him and said something like: 'My favourite!'

I was being polite and said he was welcome. The happy family pretence was very real in those moments.

I sat – and we were about to begin eating, except that Julius was still standing. He said there was a surprise, which is when he turned to the stage.

Julius: The girls had been talking about doing something like that all holiday. They had been practising in the room – and then, when Dad came back from the hospital, they asked if I could arrange something. I had a word with the manager, slipped him thirty euros, and that's what made it happen.

Emma: After dinner, the tables get cleared away and they turn the restaurant into a dance floor. It's not every night, maybe two or three times during the week, but they have a singer on who belts out hits from the seventies and eighties. It's where singles hook up and couples slobber over one another.

This time, Amy and Chloe were on the stage that's at the back of the restaurant. There was a screech from the microphone and most of the people who were eating looked to see what was going on. The stage was always empty during dinner itself, so this was something different.

The stage was behind me, so Dad, Mum, me, Victor and Liz all had to turn to look. That's important – because the only people who didn't have to twist were Julius and Daniel. The empty seats on that side were Amy and Chloe's.

The manager was holding the microphone and he said: 'We now have a special surprise for a special guest.'

Julius: The girls sang 'Granddad We Love You' for Dad. They'd been watching the video of the song on *YouTube* and learned the lyrics from that.

Emma: It was… well-intended.

…

Look, it was bad. I don't feel any happiness telling you that – but it was what it was. People were quietly going about having their evening meal and, from nowhere, two young girls got up and started singing a terrible song. The twins might have just got away with it if their singing was any good but… they were eight years old.

It wasn't great. It was like two cats being strangled.

Sorry…

Julius: Everyone loved it. Mum was clapping along and I think there was probably a tear in Dad's eyes.

Chloe: We didn't know the song. Daddy showed it to us and helped us with the words.

Amy: There were a lot of people.

Chloe: I don't want to be a singer when I grow up. There are too many words to learn.

Emma: Dad was in the chair and he'd wheeled himself a little away from the table to be able to see the stage properly. When the girls finished singing, he was definitely in tears – and banging his hands together, shouting 'More, more, more!'.

The reaction from the other tables was… muted, for want of a better word. A few people clapped, but I think most were relieved it was over. Nobody had paid thousands to come on holiday and listen to that on an evening.

Even though the singing had been bad, it was hard not to be touched. It was a classic *thought-that-counts* moment. The twins came down from the stage and weaved around the tables before they got back to Dad. They perched on either side of his chair and he gave them a huge squeeze. Mum was crying too.

Geoffrey: One of the best moments of my life – which was soon to be followed by one of the worst.

Emma: After Dad let them go, Amy and Chloe went back around to their seats and everyone sat again. Dad kept saying things like 'wonderful' and 'superb'. He said it was the best recovery present he could have hoped for – and that the girls could have as much ice cream as they wanted.

Julius: Dad had been through a lot and I know it meant a lot to him. I was so proud of them.

Emma: Dad held both hands up in the air and said: 'Let's eat!' It was like a rallying cry – and he immediately shoved his fork into his food and started to eat.

I can't remember what was on my plate. I didn't eat much on that holiday – but, whatever it was, I started to eat, too.

I remember the next bit in slow motion. I can still picture it now. Dad reached for another forkful of rice and then he started to choke. He grabbed his throat and, within a second or two, he was starting to turn purple. He was trying to talk – but the words were stuck as he gasped for air.

Mum reached towards him – and I think I probably did, too – but that's when he toppled sideways out of his chair onto the floor. There was a crack as his skull hit the ground and then a second of silence where it felt like the world had stopped and nobody seemed to know what to do.

Julius picked up a chunk of fish from Dad's plate and turned to me. His eyes were wide as he shouted…

Julius: 'What did you do?'

CHAPTER THIRTY-SEVEN

THE REAL-LIFE MAGIC

Emma: Dad has an allergy to shellfish. He's lived with it his whole life and it's something that was drummed into us as kids. Julius and I both knew about it – as did more or less everyone he knew.

There were two plates of paella at that buffet: one with pork, the other with a mixture of fish.

Julius: The staff rushed across as Dad continued to choke. I honestly thought he was going to die in that moment. Amy and Chloe were crying – but it felt like everyone was.

Mum dumped out her bag on the table and was hunting through everything inside. I didn't realise what she was doing at first, but she grabbed Dad's EPI pen, dropped to her knees and then injected it into his chest.

It was… surreal. Like real-life magic happening in front of your eyes.

Emma: Dad started to come around almost instantly. He took this really big, husky gasp and then started to breathe properly. His face went back to its normal colour and, aside from him being on the floor, it was almost as if it never happened.

Julius: One of the staff members helped me get Dad back into his chair. He was still breathing really heavily, plus there was obvious distress and disorientation. Nobody could believe what had just happened.

Daniel was on his feet and thanking people for their concern. He was telling everyone that it was all OK now. It was good of him – someone needed to do that. Dad needed space.

Daniel: I don't want any credit. I did what needed to be done.

Julius: The manager was by us at that point, but Dad managed to croak that everything was fine. Daniel thanked the staff for their quick reactions and told the rest of the diners that he hoped they enjoyed their meals. He really proved himself in those moments.

Daniel: Beth was the real hero that night, with that pen-thing. I dread to think what would have happened if she'd not been there.

Emma: When I think of it now, it all must have happened so quickly – but I also see it as this long, drawn-out moment. I remember all the facial expressions and all the small movements people made. I can still see Daniel on his feet, calming people down when it felt like things could get hysterical.

Julius: There was finally a moment of calm as I nudged Dad's chair back to the table. He was still breathing heavily and his face was swollen. He looked to the girls and assured them he was fine. He tried to make a joke of it – 'A cliff didn't get me, and neither will a fish!' but nobody laughed. The girls were terrified.

Emma: Julius picked up the plate that was in front of Dad and passed it to a waiter. The waiter was momentarily confused, wondering why someone was giving him a full plate – but he took it anyway.

It was after he left that I realised everyone around the table was looking at me.

Julius: There was a slow, dawning moment. I wanted to shield the twins from it – but they'd seen it the same as everyone else.

Emma: It was Mum's stare that hurt the most.

Julius: Daniel spoke first.

Daniel: I said: 'You've been causing trouble all week.' I think I was speaking for everyone when I said that.

Julius: There was a feeling of sadness more than anything else. Dad was blank and Mum looked broken-hearted. She was very quiet when she spoke – but we all heard it. She looked directly at Emma and said: 'You know your father is allergic to shellfish.'

Emma: I'd obviously seen what happened – and heard Julius's: 'What did you do?' – but it was only then that it properly sunk in.
    They thought I'd deliberately poisoned Dad.

Julius: Everyone around that table knew what she did.

Daniel: She knows what she did.

Liz: I don't think there was any doubt about what Emma tried to do to her father. She should have been prosecuted.

Victor: She got his food – and then he almost died. What more is there to say?

Emma: Mum was almost whispering when she was talking to me. She said: 'I think you should leave the table now.'
    I wanted to defend myself, but, as I looked around, I realised she was saying what everyone else was thinking. Dad was still

struggling to breathe – but he was staring at the empty space on the table in front of him. Nobody wanted me there, so I did the only thing I could. I stood up and I left.

CHAPTER THIRTY-EIGHT

DAY SEVEN

IT'S A SECRET

Emma: I didn't leave the cottage until five minutes to midday the next day. I heard Mum and Dad get back to their cottage the night before – and I heard them moving around in the morning – but nobody knocked on my door.

Daniel: Everyone had breakfast together on the final day – and it was a joyous occasion. It was nice to be surrounded by people who enjoyed one another's company and who were all on the same page.

That's how the entire holiday should have been.

Emma: I don't know if this happened – but I'd assume Dad went out in a car that morning to collect whatever it was he had to collect, from wherever it was he had to collect it. He wouldn't have left the island without completing the one job he went there to do.

I'd almost forgotten about it by the time I got to the lobby. There were taxis ordered that were due to take us back to the airport. They weren't coming until 12.30 – but I had to check out at 12, which meant thirty awkward minutes in that lobby.

Mum and Dad were by the main hotel doors, while the twins were nearby on a small sofa, playing on their iPads. Daniel and Liz were hanging around, but there was no sign of Julius.

I sat on a chair across the lobby from everyone, trying not to make eye contact. I had a magazine that I was going to read – or at least pretend to – but then Victor plopped himself down on the arm of my chair.

Victor: I was trying to be friendly. Nobody else was talking to her. I said: 'Your holiday went about as well as mine.'

Emma: I replied: 'Your wife dumped you and went home almost as soon as she arrived.'

Victor: 'Exactly!'

Emma: He laughed and said that, in many ways, it meant he'd had a better time of it than me. I suppose it was hard to disagree, though I didn't feel much like laughing. He'd had a strange sort of reinvention in those few days he'd been AWOL. Singledom and island life probably suited him more than it would most people. I guess it's easier when you're a forty-year-old man living off daddy's money.

He rested a hand on my knee and said: 'I'm here for you.'

I gave him the full '*Really?*' treatment and he shrugged it away.

Victor: Worth a go, wasn't it?

Emma: I told him that I wasn't interested and then picked up my case and headed across towards the twins. There was still no sign of Julius – and if Mum or Dad wanted to tell me to leave the girls alone, then they could at least do it in front of their faces.

As it was, nobody bothered me. I put my case on the floor and sat on it in front of Amy and Chloe. I thought for a moment that they'd continue playing on their iPads. They didn't put them down immediately, but, after a few seconds, Amy lowered hers first. She glanced across to the door and then said, very quietly: 'Daddy says we're not supposed to be talking to you.'

Daniel: The absolute gall of that girl – after what she'd tried to pull the night before.

Emma: Chloe had put down her iPad by that point too – and both girls were looking at me. They were dressed identically, with matching tops that said 'Galanikos Girl' across the front.

I told them that if I didn't see them for a while, then it wasn't because I didn't want to. I explained that their dad and I had had a bit of a falling out, but that I hoped, in time, we'd make it up and I'd be able to spend time with them again.

Amy said: 'Is that like how Mum and Dad have had a falling out?' – but I wasn't sure what to say. Julius and Simone were divorcing, which was a lot past a 'falling out'. Then again, I wasn't sure how much I would be talking to my family in future.

I probably repeated that I hoped we'd work things out, but that, if not, I wanted them to know it was nothing they'd done.

I was going to leave it at that, but, as I went to move, the two girls exchanged a glance that was so full of self-awareness that it left me stumbling a bit.

They'd done something similar on the cliff when I'd found them. Amy had started to say: 'The other night…' when that look had passed between them the first time and she'd stopped herself. In the end, she'd told me she'd overheard her mum saying that Julius had lost his job.

On the cliffs, I thought they were entrusting me with that secret, but, in that moment in the lobby, I realised there was something else and that the girls were asking each other's permission to share it.

Amy whispered: 'Go on,' but Chloe was still staring wide-eyed at her sister.

I said: 'What is it?' and Amy replied: 'It's a secret.'

I waited and it was like they were having a long back and forth, even though neither of them spoke a word.

I said: 'It sounds like you want to tell me…' – and they looked to each other one more time before Chloe finally said it.

Chloe: I don't know what I told Auntie Emma in the lobby.

Amy: I don't know either.

Emma: Chloe said: 'We woke up on the first night.'

And then Amy added: 'When Granddad fell.'

There was a pause and I could picture those two little girls sitting on the secret for almost a week, desperate to tell someone. They'd almost told me on the cliffs and they probably knew this was the last opportunity.

Chloe finished the sentence – and she said: 'Daddy wasn't there.'

CHAPTER THIRTY-NINE

THE EVEN SMALLER THINGS

Julius: I don't know if Emma made them say that, or if she made it up all by herself. If either of the girls *did* say that I was out of the room on that first night, then all I can say is that I would have been in the bathroom, or possibly on the balcony. I never left the room.

Emma: Have you ever done a Sudoku puzzle? It's the one where there are nine boxes of nine squares – and you have to fit numbers one to nine into each row and column.

When you're doing one, there comes a point where you're so far into completing the puzzle that the final ten or twenty numbers almost write themselves into the grid. You've done all the hard work – and it's that which makes the final bit seem so easy.

It felt like that when the twins told me that Julius was out of the room. I'd had so many little bits of information – and then this last little piece suddenly made the rest make sense.

It was past checkout time, but Julius wasn't in the lobby. I asked the twins where their dad was, and Amy said he was still packing in the room, so I took the lift upstairs and headed along to his door.

There was a maid's trolley towards the other end of the corridor, but the floor was otherwise quiet. I almost knocked before I realised that the latch had been locked in place and that Julius's door was open a crack.

Julius: It had been a busy morning. Everyone had breakfast together, except my sister, and then the girls had wanted one more hour at the pool before we went back up to pack. I'd sorted them out first but hadn't quite finished my own packing. I was only running a few minutes late – and the taxis weren't due until half-past twelve anyway.

Emma: Julius's suitcase was open on the bed and there was a scattering of clothes and other things around the room. It was a bit of a mess – and I couldn't see Julius. I moved inside, looking around the corners to see if he was in there somewhere.

I found myself over by the balcony door, which was open – although Julius wasn't out there either. The door to the bathroom was closed and I figured that was the only place he could be. I was about to move, which is when I spotted the bin at the foot of the bed. It was almost full, mainly of food wrappers – but sitting on top was the necklace that Julius had bought at the airport on the first day.

I picked it up and shook it around – and it made the same whooshing sound that it had when we were in the shop. The noise that had entertained the girls so much. Julius had been wearing it at the first dinner, and then I'd not seen it since. I'd not even thought about it.

The necklace was still in my hand when I looked up and realised Julius was standing in the middle of the room.

He said: 'What are you doing?'

Julius: That's a reasonable question, isn't it? I'd not heard her come into the room and then, all of a sudden, I come out of the toilet and she's standing right there.

Emma: When we were in the hospital, Dad said that he was looking out over the cliffs and then he heard the wind whistling before he fell.

It felt like a really normal observation, except that I had walked to the hotel next door that night and didn't remember it being windy. I said that to Julius and then rattled the necklace, which made a sort of cooing, low hum.

Like a gentle wind on a quiet night.

Julius: Emma said: 'I have to tell you something.'

Emma: After I rattled the necklace, Julius said: 'What are you talking about?'

I told him about the 'Who benefits?' line that Scott had mentioned. Scott always thought Dad had something to do with his own father's death because it was my dad who benefitted the most.

Julius hadn't known about the documentary and Scott at that point. It was all news to him and he didn't know what to make of it.

Julius: She said: 'I need the money.' I said: 'What money?' – and Emma replied: 'Dad's money.'

Emma: Scott got that thought stuck in my head, except that I'd missed the most obvious thing. Mum didn't have long to live, so if Dad also died, who was next in line? It wasn't me. It would be the favourite son… the one who'd lost his highly paid banking job and not told his parents.

It would have been Julius who inherited the business.

There was literally nobody who would have benefitted more than my brother.

Julius: I was confused. I didn't know what money she was talking about, but Emma kept saying: 'Dad's money' as if that meant something.

She asked if I could lend her 'ten- or twenty-thousand', that she wanted to get her own place and that she couldn't afford it on her shop wages. She kept saying: 'You earn loads; you can afford it.'

Emma: I kept thinking of the night before, when Dad had been poisoned. I was so certain I'd put the pork paella on his plate. As certain as a person can be. I wouldn't have made that mistake.

But Julius was right behind me in the line and there was rice on his plates. When the twins were on stage everyone had to turn, except Julius and Daniel. Daniel was further along the table, so perhaps he didn't notice – or maybe he didn't care.

Julius could have easily switched a plate with Dad in that time. It was Julius who called the waiter across and got rid of it so quickly afterwards. If I'd been paying better attention, I bet I would have noticed that Julius had the pork paella in front of him.

Julius: Emma was getting upset at this point. She said: 'I had to do something. I can't live like this any longer.' I asked what she meant and she said that Mum didn't have long to live. When Dad died, everything would be split between us – but she couldn't wait that long.

Emma: Then there were the even smaller things. Julius said that Daniel had disapproved of some of Dad's spending at the airport – but I'd not seen any of that. In fact, I couldn't understand why Daniel would care. He'd got a free holiday out of things.

The only person who'd mentioned Dad's spending was Julius. In the taxi on the way back from the hospital the first time, he'd said that Dad had been throwing money around since Mum got her diagnosis. I didn't care – but he did. It meant it would be less left over to inherit.

Julius: It took me a while to catch on. I thought it might have been a mistake with the meal the night before, but I said: 'Are you saying you tried to kill Dad?'

Emma stared at me with those cold, determined eyes of hers. She said: 'It would be better for both of us, wouldn't it?'

Emma: I saw Julius for who he was in that moment. On that first night, when he'd said that everything he did was for the girls, it felt so fake – and that's because it was. It was always about him.

Julius: I saw Emma for who she was in that moment. Heartless and cold. Everything's always about her.

Emma: I laid all those things out to him. It wasn't evidence as such – the necklace that sounded like wind, the fact Julius was out of the room on the night Dad fell, his lost job, the opportunity to switch plates… and the fact that Julius would be the person who benefitted from our parents' deaths.

Julius listened, but he wasn't replying to anything. He turned and walked across the room. I thought he was leaving – but he unlatched the hinge and let the door swing closed – then he turned and strode back towards me.

I didn't know what was going to happen in that moment. I said something like: 'You were going to let everyone think that I'd poisoned Dad…?'

I thought he'd reply, but he was silent. Instead, he kept moving faster and faster towards me. I stepped backwards and he shouted: 'You don't have to do this.'

I had no idea what was going on. He was only a few steps from me and I replied: 'Do what?'

He was still shouting, probably even louder at this point and he yelled: 'You've got so much to live for.'

Everything happened in a flash after that. He shouldered into me, shoving me backwards towards the railing of the balcony – and that's when I realised he was trying to make it sound like I was suicidal.

I said: 'No' – but it was too late. He was already grabbing my legs and trying to throw me over the top.

Julius: Emma had basically confessed that she tried to kill Dad. She'd failed to such a degree that she'd damaged any relationship she was ever going to have with the family again.

I saw what was going to happen a moment before it did. She lunged towards the balcony. I shouted something like: 'You don't have to do this' – as I was trying to hold onto her.

We burst through the balcony doors and I was trying to say that she had so much to live for. She seemed so determined to throw herself off and it was all I could do to stop her. It felt like she wanted to die – and I was desperately trying to stop her.

Emma: He was trying to kill me and, as the railing dug into my back, my feet came off the floor. His eyes weren't wild or wide. He was calm and he knew exactly what he was doing.

I could feel him lifting me; shoving harder into my chest until all that was left was for me to go backwards over the rail and fall to the ground below.

CHAPTER FORTY

THE SPOILER ALERT

Emma: Spoiler alert: I didn't die.

You should have probably had someone else tell all my parts, then there would have been a bit more drama here. I could have popped up with a big *ta-da* moment…

Julius: We were struggling on the balcony and I was trying to pull her back.

Emma: I genuinely did believe I was going to die in that moment. I think I was ready for it. It's not as if I was suicidal, but I was probably accepting. He was stronger than me and a sort of calmness came over me…

…

It was only momentary – then I decided that there was no way I was letting him get away with it.

Julius: She was flailing and kicking.

Emma: I flailed and kicked, all right. I remembered the times I'd seen Julius wince because of his side – and I booted him as hard as I could right in the soft bit above his hip.

Julius: I don't want people saying I'm a hero. I only did what anyone else would have done in that situation. I saved my sister's life.

Emma: He crumpled like a broken ironing board – and we both fell forward, away from the railing. He tried to grab my ankle but could barely get his breath – so I punched him one more time in the side and then made a run for the door.

Julius: Emma was still flailing – but there was a moment when I looked up and realised the maid had come into the room. She will back me up on this.

Emma: I didn't get to the door because the maid was there. She was staring out towards the balcony and I think she'd seen everything. She can back me up on this.

Rosa Makos (hotel maid, through an interpreter): I saw two people fighting on the balcony – a man and a woman. The woman was kicking and throwing her arms – *bam-bam-bam*. The two of them fell away from the balcony and landed on the floor, then the woman ran towards me.

That is all I saw.

Emma: Julius was stumbling behind me, but we both stopped when we saw the maid. It felt like we'd been play-fighting as kids and that Mum had walked in… except it was so much more serious than that.

Julius: Thank god the maid was there. I really think Emma would have tried to jump a second time if it hadn't been for her.

Emma: Julius was struggling to breathe – and he didn't do much to stop me as I left the room. I went to the lifts, pressed the button for the ground floor, and then rode it down on my own.

Everyone was still sitting or standing with their cases, waiting for their buses or taxis.

Nothing had changed… but everything had.

I walked across to take my case from the floor next to the twins – but Mum must have seen something in me. We'd not spoken since she told me to leave the table the night before – but she came across and took my arm before asking if everything was all right.

I looked her right in the eyes and I thought about her diagnosis, and I thought about the family.

There was Dad, who had arranged this entire thing in order to rob a bank with a fake driving licence with the details of a man who was dead. It might even have been a man that he had killed.

There was my mother, who endured and tolerated all this, even though she was dying.

There was my brother, who had probably tried to kill our dad to protect an inheritance. Who had literally just tried to kill his sister.

Then there was me. The woman who killed her baby son because she'd had too much to drink and then got into a car. The woman whose husband left because he couldn't bear to look at her any longer.

And I thought about what I should say.

Julius: It was only later that I found out Emma supposedly has an alibi for that night Dad fell. It took me a while to put things together – but then I found out the person giving her the alibi is the person who works for you.

Emma keeps talking about who benefits – but it's you, isn't it? It's Garibaldi Media. It's *your* movie.

And that's when I put it all together.

There are a few things that could have happened that first night. Option one is that Dad fell. I don't believe that – and neither does he any longer.

Second, Emma used Paul as an alibi and then snuck out of the room when he was asleep. She stumbled across Dad on the cliffs and took her chance. It's not that hard to believe. She was never the favourite child and then, after what happened with her son, Dad never looked at her the same way again.

Third – and I think this is the most likely – Emma and Paul were in on it together. You were making a documentary and he thought it would make for a better story. I know you might not want to believe it, but there it is.

Do you have a better version of events?

Emma: I wondered if I should tell her about all the things I'd just challenged Julius about. If I should mention what had just happened upstairs on the balcony.

I wondered if she would believe me – because it would always come down to my word versus his. My word versus her favourite's.

The lift pinged and Julius came out, dragging his case behind him. He walked through the lobby, focused only on me, with the wheels of his case bumping across the tiled grooves. And then, suddenly, he was in front of us: a triangle of me, him and Mum. He was breathing loudly, still struggling for breath, and he said: 'We're family.'

I know it doesn't sound like much – but it was a declaration of war. As if he was saying: 'This is us and this is what we do. Like it or leave.'

It was so simple and all I could reply was: 'Yes. Yes, we are.'

And we *are* family – except, if I had to like it or leave, then there was only ever going to be one decision.

AUTHOR'S NOTE

After the McGinley and Dorsey families arrived back in the UK, Emma emailed the team at Garibaldi Media, asking if she could tell her story. Much of this book came from interviews done in the three weeks immediately after that email was sent.

Following her claims, a decision was taken that the original documentary being made about the death of Alan Lee could not be completed without including the happenings from nine years later.

The truth was that the original plans were going nowhere. The cause of Alan Lee's death is still considered an accident, with nothing other than circumstantial evidence able to show anything different. In all the work already done by the crew, it was felt they could still salvage something – and that was Emma's story.

Alongside that decision, it was mutually agreed that Paul Bosley should be assigned to other projects at Garibaldi Media. His connection to Emma was such that the rest of the crew felt the appearance of bias could disrupt the project. He agreed with this decision, even though he made it clear to his colleagues that he and Emma were not in contact now they had returned to the UK.

After Emma told her side of the story, open invitations were made to everyone else involved as to whether they wanted to give their version of events. Over the course of around six months, many interviews were given on camera. Everything you have read on the pages before this are what came from those recordings. In case of confusion or speculation, Bethan McGinley was too ill to take part.

It was around that six-month mark that my friend, whom I'll name Frank, showed me a very rough cut of the movie. It was almost five hours long at that point.

In an earlier chapter, Emma described Frank as having 'a big mouth and a fat arse and a stupid walk', but, in his defence, I've never seen him do a stupid walk.

Frank asked my opinion about the footage, wondering if there was something there.

I have written numerous crime fiction books over the years, inventing many characters, but I told him what I'm happy to write here: Emma McGinley is one of the most fascinating people I've ever come across. If you've been charmed or dismayed by anything in this book, then I cannot stress enough how much more can be taken from watching the footage. It feels as if Emma is talking to you and only you. That there is no screen and that you're in the room with her.

She is hypnotic.

There was one other question that Frank had for me: Who do you believe?

I had to think on that issue – and, at the time, thought I had an answer.

I believed Emma.

Julius says she tried to kill her father because she wanted her parents' inheritance – but nothing about Emma makes me think she has any interest in money. She chose to work in a shop for very little, simply because it meant she could be with her friend.

Meanwhile, I believed her that Julius's own daughters said he was out of the hotel room on the night their father fell. I believed her about the sound of the necklace, compared to the sound their father heard on the cliffs. I believed her that Julius tried to get rid of it.

Other things are on record. Julius's 'unreasonable behaviour' was cited in his divorce, which, combined with his loss of job, meant that money really was an issue for him. Any inheritance would have undoubtedly helped with his financial issues – and he was likely next in line.

If Emma is believed on those things, then she has to be believed when she says she did not knowingly put shellfish on her father's plate at the final meal. That means she either did so accidentally, or that Julius really did switch plates when everyone's backs were turned.

Similarly, if she is believed on those things, then her brother really did try to push her from the balcony to cover up the things he'd done.

And I believed Emma.

The past tense of 'believed' is very important, though, because, ten days later, a bombshell hit – and everything I thought I knew changed.

Frank and I live in a different time zone and, when I woke up to his email explaining what had gone on, I genuinely dropped my phone. I know that sounds like a cliché – and I'm not usually a clumsy person – but it was like the Earth had started spinning the other way. After watching those near five hours of footage, Frank's movie had wedged itself into my brain. I felt like I knew every one of Emma, Julius, Daniel and the rest.

At some point around that all-important six-month mark, Paul Bosley took a week of annual leave. There was nothing unusual about this and he told colleagues at Garibaldi Media he was visiting Spain to get a bit of sun.

Paul did not return to work at the conclusion of his break.

Through those six months, Emma had largely been ostracised from her family – a fact that has been confirmed by them. Her father and brother have not spoken to her since returning from Galanikos. The only contact with her mother was a short phone call around a week after they returned. I do not know the content of that call, nor do I want to.

Despite that, Emma had been a keen participant in the process of making the movie. She sat for many interviews and was happy to come back to clarify claims and points made by others. It is for this reason that things can sometimes appear as if people are directly responding to others within these pages.

At the same time as Paul went on holiday, Emma stopped communicating with the Garibaldi Media team. She did not respond to emails or phone calls. Upon contacting her family and Tina, it quickly became clear that none of them knew where she was.

As part of its work in investigating old crimes, Garibaldi Media has a network of private investigators who carry out jobs for them. Much of this involves sourcing documents or, occasionally, finding a person.

It was six days after Paul was due back from holiday that Frank emailed me.

Emma McGinley and Paul Bosley married in secret in a place that I will not name. There were no members of either of their families present and attempts to contact the named witnesses have proved fruitless. I have personally seen a copy of the wedding certificate and am happy with its veracity.

Neither Paul nor Emma have been in contact with anyone at Garibaldi Media since that moment. As far as I know, neither have contacted their families and friends since. I have heard rumours of where they might now be living, but, if I'm honest, I'm not sure it's any of my business as to where they are.

It is because of this that funding for Frank's movie fell through. The reasoning was that, if Paul was compromised by Emma, then there is a chance the movie could be.

Frank and the rest of his crew made the argument that Paul had been isolated away from the editing and filming – and that there was no problem. This was dismissed by the people who put up the original funding for the project.

I disagree with Frank on this matter. He thought the movie could still go ahead, I'm not sure that it could.

Not then, anyway.

Emma and Julius have such conflicting versions of what happened that they cannot be reconciled. However, Julius's claim that Emma and Paul were 'in it together', or that he was 'covering for her' is something that has been complicated by Emma and Paul's disappearance and marriage.

That does not mean I necessarily believe Julius's version to be true – but that the project likely *was* compromised. This is especially the case as Paul told his colleagues that he and Emma had no relationship after returning from the island. In short, why lie?

There is also the email.

Approximately three weeks before Paul went on holiday, an email was sent from his Garibaldi Media work address to the same Gmail account that Emma had been using to communicate with Frank.

The only reason this was uncovered was due to a forensic crawl of Paul's work emails in the week he was seemingly missing. Colleagues were worried about him and searching for clues as to where he might be. At the time this email was uncovered, nobody involved in this story was aware that Paul and Emma were still in contact.

There is an assumption that Paul sent this email by accident, when he meant to use his own personal account.

This is the email:

From: Paul Bosley

To: Emma McGinley

Subject: J ints

E!

Things looking good here. J interviews finished today but you def sound more believable. Talk later.

X

Paul

It seems a fair assumption that 'J' means Julius, but, as with so many things in this story, different things can be read into this email, depending on who you believe.

The only certainty is that Emma and Paul *were* in contact with one another – and that Paul was keeping a check on the interviews, even though he was working in a different department.

Through email, I gave Julius a right to reply about everything that happened since Emma disappeared. Edited and reprinted with permission, this is his response:

Julius: Emma eloping to marry the guy from the film crew shows you that everything I said was true. It doesn't matter if you believe they were in it together, or if you think she seduced him and got him to cover for her. All that matters is that she showed her true colours. She tried to kill our dad because she wanted his money – and that's a fact.

Garibaldi Media was Frank's company but, with things as they were, he was forced to move onto other ventures. He has since worked on at least one big-name documentary of which you have likely heard – and is currently hard at work on another. I have shielded his name – and changed the name of his company – solely to protect his professional reputation. Many in the film-making industry know who he is – but he is a private man and deserves to be left alone.

As a project, Frank's movie was dead – however, he gave me a hard drive filled with terabytes of unedited, raw video. He told me I could do with it whatever I wanted. Everyone involved had signed disclaimers, so there were, and are, no privacy or legal issues to be considered.

I thought about turning this story into some sort of fiction novel, perhaps like my others. I could have written it first-person from Emma's point-of-view, or perhaps third with a bit of Julius involved. The problem was, every time I sat down, nothing came out. These characters had such unique voices that I realised there was no point in trying to ape them.

Over the course of many, many months, I watched and re-watched every second of footage and transcribed everything. I managed to work those interviews into something approximating a chronological order. What's left, I believe, is as accurate a story as is likely to be told of what happened on Galanikos.

I have a confession to make here: I have never visited the island and, with the exception of Paul, I haven't met anyone who gave an interview for this story. My only meeting with Paul was when I was visiting the UK. He was on a night out with Frank and some of the other Garibaldi Media team, on which I tagged along. We might have exchanged a few words, but, honestly, I don't remember him.

If you feel like you know the island of Galanikos, or even that you know the people involved, it is solely because of the wit and verbal dexterity of everyone who was interviewed. I thank them for that.

After I finished writing everything you've read, I sent it off to my editor in London. My phone rang approximately nine hours later, at 2.35 in the morning. I was asleep and grabbed my phone from the side table. Through groggy eyes, I didn't take in a name on the screen, I simply answered – expecting bad news. Instead, it was my editor.

'What do you think happened?'

It might have been early in the morning, but I understand that desperation to know. *I* want to know.

It's not only a question of who did what, but whether anything was done at all. Did Geoff fall, or was he pushed? And, if he was pushed, then by whom? Did Emma attempt to poison her father, or was it Julius? Or was it an honest mistake? Did Emma invent the story of the hidden money, or was it a genuine truth that ripped apart all those years of childhood memories?

In short, it is about faith.

Do you believe Julius, or do you believe Emma?

The main fact I can give you is that the police investigation was closed with no charges made. In the eyes of the law, Geoffrey McGinley fell unaided from that cliff, in the same way Alan Lee had nine years before.

It was an accident.

In addition, I have uncovered no proof that the Bank of Galanikos exists, but then, as leaks like the Panama Papers showed, that doesn't mean it isn't there.

What is clear is that, with a handful of exceptions, more or less everyone interviewed for this project has told lies.

The biggest exception is Rosa the maid. Her account can corroborate either of Julius or Emma's versions of events, depending on who you believe in the first place.

And that, I suppose is the biggest problem. There is no version of this story that involves absolutes. Nobody who is blameless.

I've often wondered what this story actually is. Is it a true crime tale, or is it an examination of family, jealousy and grief? Maybe it's all of those things? Or maybe, after everything, it is a simple tale of someone who pushed their father off a cliff and got away with it.

I want to give almost the last word to Tina, who owns the vintage clothes shop where Emma once worked. She doesn't feature a lot in this story – but her testimony is, I think, incredibly powerful.

As I was coming towards the end of this project, I emailed Tina to ask if she might like to add anything to the initial interview she gave. Everything she spoke in the first instance was said *before* Emma eloped – and it felt like she, perhaps more than anyone, had an unfinished story.

I sent Tina the transcript of what she'd said before and, with her permission, this is her emailed reply:

Tina: The line that stands out to me is: 'She's the best person I know, but she has a really good way of hiding it.'

I remember saying that about Emma and wondering if it was too harsh. At the time, I assumed there was going to be a documentary and, if it made the cut, Emma would see that. I didn't want to upset her – but I also didn't want to be dishonest.

I think everything that's happened since those interviews probably back up what I said. Emma's exactly the sort of person I would imagine eloping. I can see her being seduced by love – and then running away to chase it.

I miss my friend.

We talked more or less every day and then, all of a sudden, I haven't heard from her in over a year. I've replayed the conversations we had and wondered if it's something I said, or did. Maybe it is?

I suppose I'd like to think that Emma found a way to escape everything from her past and make a new start. She was never going to get past everything that happened to her if she remained around all the people she knew from before.

If I'm collateral damage because she had to save herself, then I can live with that. I always said that Emma saved herself.

I don't wish Emma any ill will, in fact I wish her the opposite. I hope she's happy. She deserves it and, if anything comes from your book, I hope it's a true reflection of who she is.

There's a natural human desire for closure and definite answers – but the truth is that life isn't like that. Even in a case that goes all the way to court, much of what goes in front of a jury is one person's word versus another's. We can all play detective and ask what we might have done differently, or think of the questions we'd have wanted asking. We can look at all the evidence – and then decide who we believe.

Except, even when we do that, the person sitting to our side might well come to a completely different conclusion, despite the identical evidence.

I have my own, conflicting, ideas about what happened on the island, but my version is no more valid than yours. You now know as much as me – and I'm more than happy for you to tell me your theories.

If you liked this book, then please tell your friends and your family. Leave a review somewhere that another reader might see it. Post about it on your social network of choice.

The only way the *After the Accident* footage is ever likely to see the light of day will be if enough people say they want to see the movie. Although it's not her real name, Emma McGinley is an extraordinary person – and, one day, I hope you all get to see that for yourself.

I wrote above that I wasn't sure whether this book is a true crime tale, or an examination of family, jealousy and grief. It still could be any, or all, of those things but maybe, just maybe, it's a story of love.

I will now give the final word to Emma. When Paul sent that email from his work account, Emma replied. Her response is included below.

Thanks for reading,

- Kerry Wilkinson

THE FINAL WORD

From: Emma McGinley

To: Paul Bosley

Subject: re: J ints

P!

I love you.

X

E!

After the Accident **publishing team**

Editorial
Claire Bord
Ellen Gleeson

Line edits and copyeditor
Jade Craddock

Proofreader
Loma Halden

Production
Alexandra Holmes
Caolinn Douglas
Ramesh Kumar

Design
Lisa Horton

Marketing
Alex Crow
Jules Macadam
Hannah Deuce

Publicity
Kim Nash

Distribution
Chris Lucraft
Marina Valles

Audio
Leodora Darlington
Arran Dutton & Dave Perry –
    Audio Factory
Alison Campbell
Alan Medcroft
Martin Reeve
Andrew Kingston
Diana Croft
Tamsin Kennard

Rights and contracts
Peta Nightingale
Martina Arzu